THE XENO MANIFESTO

RECLAMATION

BRYSEN MANN

 **Time Matters Publishing**
www.brysenmann.com

ISBN
978-1-7753639-0-3 (Paperback)
978-1-7753639-1-0 (eBook)

DEDICATION

To those who are willing to accept that
the face of reality is about to change.

ACKNOWLEDGEMENTS

To those I have not thanked before, you know
who you are and I am in your debt.

PROLOGUE

Sergeant James Richard McCulley tries to get as comfortable as he can. It's a struggle considering his bulky frame is imbedded in the cab of a Humvee Slantback suspended five thousand feet in the air, by a sling attached to a CH-47 Chinook Helicopter. He has the engine running with the heater blasting, trying to keep warm and because he needs to hit the ground running when he touches down.

It's just after sunrise as they make the aerial ascent up the mountain. Earlier recons have provided strong evidence that this mountain's cave system is a suspected Tsiatko stronghold. There should be little resistance as these Beings prefer the night.

He looks back at the quarter kiloton hydrogen bomb stowed behind him in the cargo area. It's encased in a steel cage that's been welded in place. There's no access to it and it's on a pre-set timer. The doors of the Humvee have been welded shut and the windshield has been replaced with a sheet of steel except for an eight by twelve inch pane of bullet proof glass directly in front of the driver's seat. He's encased in his own tomb. There's no escape for him. He knows this is a one way trip. He had volunteered for it and accepts the fact that virtually no one will ever know of this mission or his sacrifice. Belette made sure of that.

"Jimmy, everything good?" The helicopter pilot asks through the headset.

"Yea, as good as it can get. You boys remember…its drop and run for you guys. You're not gonna have much time to clear out of here, away from the blast zone." Jimmy replies.

"We hear you. Oorah! You get those motherfuckers! You hear me Jimmy?! Get every last one of those soma bitches!"

"I hear you." Is his whispered reply.

Ten minutes of silence later the pilot announces, "We're here Jimmy." As he maintains the Chinook in a hovering position with his cargo dangling just six feet above a semi-flat area, fifty feet from the cave entrance.

"Release me." Jimmy orders and everything rattles as his personal mausoleum hits the rock strewn granite landing site.

"Rock n roll, it's been an honor and a privilege serving with you Jimmy." The pilot replies as he flies away.

Sergeant McCully doesn't respond, he's already stomping on the gas pedal which automatically locks the vehicle in at thirty miles per hour. He needs the speed as, a few yards into the Lake Cave, there's a ten foot drop to its floor and he needs the momentum to clear it. He flips a switch and twelve cage protected, powerful floodlights mounted on the front of the Slantback light up the interior of the dark cavern. The Humvee hits the cave floor hard, careens and bounces off the cave walls as there's little traction on the rough, wet and muddy terrain. It's getting banged up as he follows the winding pathway but that doesn't matter, his goal is to penetrate as far into the mountain as quickly as he can. Sixty seconds later and a half mile into Lake Cave, his progress hasn't been challenged.

"What the fuck?!" He yells as two powerful hairy arms reach in through the cab, as if it wasn't even there. He involuntarily hollers as he's being extracted through the very fabric of the steel and composite reinforced protective shield of the Humvee. He's now outside the vehicle, huge shaggy arms press him against the hairy body of the creature that now has him; holding him tight as if to protect him. His senses are immune to the foul odour of musk, ammonia, dirt and the reek of skunk emitting from his keeper as he watches helplessly as the driverless Humvee plows into a wall. The impact shatters most of the floodlights while the engine still revs and the wheels churn fruitlessly trying to make headway against the impenetrable solid stone barrier. A multitude of Tsiatko, emerge from the cave walls and surround it. A burst of brilliant white light shatters the dark of the cave. It's the fusion reaction of the hydrogen bomb as it detonates and Jimmy has no time to reflect on what's just happened to him.

This event happened at eight thirty-two in the morning, May eighteenth, nineteen-eighty and the location was Mount St. Helens, Washington State.

CHAPTER ONE

"I agree to your terms." says Brother who is the Tsiatko leader that Frank Smirnov has just sworn allegiance to "But that one," Indicating Frank's partner Zachariah Allmass, "Will not be allowed free rein."

"Works for me." Frank replies as he brushes past Zach and heads for his tent set up around the corner of the cavern they're in, deep beneath the peak of Mt. Rainier. He needs solitude to investigate what's hidden in the pouch that Mr. H used to transport the Orb.

Zach attempts to follow but a wall of Tsiatko block his way once more and he has no choice but to take a seat on a rock again. He wraps himself in his sleeping bag. "Frank!" Zach shouts, "Frank…you can't leave me here like this! Do you know what you agreed to?!"

Frank's already in his tent, digging out the pouch. He extracts what turns out to be a small envelope from the hidden pocket.

Zach is still yelling to him. "Frank?! Christ…Frank?! Jesus…what the fuck! This is crazy! You want a mongrel like you, a preacher's son and, what…a bunch of mythical creatures, to take on the Committee?! Are you nuts?! For what, possibly eliminate the entire human civilization…forever?!"

His words are falling on deaf ears. On the envelope is written: *To my redeemer, Mr. H*

Frank knows the handwriting. It's Mr. H's, his guardian angel to a certain degree. There's a folded sheet of paper inside the envelope.

I have hidden this note away trusting, no, knowing you would one day be led to the Orb. I could not risk including this in my journals as I did not know if they would be discovered by friend or foe.

Your creation has been foretold by the previous occupations, but the timeline for it was skewed by the Roswell crash. You are a parameter of this experiment that must be maintained to ensure man's successful occupation here. I learned this from the Orb's data logs but, you arrived over fifty years earlier than the Handlers' scheduled timeline for you.

Somehow the Committee learnt how critical your existence is, even though I was successful in deleting this fact from the Orb's memory. They were intent on impeding your entry into this world, so I recruited the Solomons specifically to complete your inception, regardless of the schedule for your arrival.

The Committee discovered this, not knowing my participation and killed the Solomons to halt the procedure, unaware you already existed, safely tucked away in another's womb.

You must believe this… there is hope for man on this world. Trust no one, not even the Tsiatko.

Frank pops his head outside the tent to make sure there're no Tsiatko watching over him, not that he'd be absolutely sure with their constant disappearing acts. There's nothing. He plops down and reads Mr. H's note one more time. He's not sure what to think. He tears the envelope and note into small pieces, chewing each piece and washing them down with shots from his water bottle, shaking his head in disbelief with every swallow. Frank's beginning to think he's fucked.

Zach scans around. The sounds of the steam echo as mist clouds of vapour shoot out from the small fumaroles in the cave floor and he watches as the lights dance across the ceiling and walls of the immense circular cavern emanating from the blue glow of the Orb, its radiance further reflected by the quartz boulder it's nested on. Under different circumstances he may have considered all of this a beautiful image but in this instance, it is tainted by the sight and disgusting smell of the gigantic Tsiatko scattered around him. They're still scowling at him like they're ready to rip him apart and Brother's recent comments have done nothing to help matters. He sits dejected on his rock stool, staring at the Orb. So close yet so far. He's still bewildered why Frank saved him from the Tsiatko's wrath and more perplexed as to what Frank is really up to. Zach did have his own game plan for the Orb but Frank's actions have left him hanging … alive, but hanging. He had a Plan A and B but no Plan C. Zach's beginning to think he's fucked.

Frank's not sure what his next course of action should be. He had such high hopes when he encountered the Tsiatko, the very creatures Zach said he was genetically related to. He immediately felt at ease with them and actually began to believe he was part of something, had a distant family even though there's nothing one could consider a family resemblance. Mr. H's message has now dashed any ideas he had of fitting into something, anything and Frank doesn't doubt his words of wisdom and warning. Is he the one to save mankind and can it really be something foretold? This is like a weird version of the Matrix, really, what can he do to save mankind? But he knows, by the way circumstances have unfolded since he stumbled across Mr. H's remains, anything seems possible. And regardless of how much Frank dwells on it, he needs Zach. As little as he trusts him, he can't move forward without him as Frank knows nothing about the Committee or the capabilities of the Tsiatko's unknown powers that Brother said they're prepared to unleash on the world. He has no other choice and heads back to the cavern where Zach and the Orb are.

"Frank, c'mon, you gotta get me out of here." Zach pleads from behind the bodies of his Tsiatko sentries.

Frank waves him quiet and approaches one of the Tsiatko guarding Zach. "Where's Brother?" He asks. "I need to speak with him."

The Tsiatko turns and nods to another who leaves. Frank waits, trying to ignore Zach.

"Frank, what the fuck?" Zach asks as he stands, throwing his sleeping bag across the rock he was seated on. He peeks between two of the Tsiatko. "You can't leave me here like this … I can help. Seriously."

"Zach, shut the fuck up. I've got this." Frank warns him.

Momentarily Brother enters. "You requested me?" He asks.

"Brother, I have vowed that I would assist but you have to admit that even with what Tsiatko are under your command and the powers you possess, must realize that facing a population of humans that number in the billions will be a daunting task.

"I do. We are prepared to make whatever sacrifices are required." He replies.

"And I understand that but, with his help," Frank says pointing to Zach, "We can accomplish so much more with little risk to those who look to you for leadership. The Committee is powerful with resources that are worldwide and weaponry that can result in high casualties, even with your abilities. You must know this. They'll not hold back if it comes to an actual war."

"What do you propose?" Brother asks.

"To start, I only want some time alone with Zach to discuss our options as he knows the Committee so well."

"And you believe he will be truthful as to what he knows and his true intentions? I think not." Brother answers.

"Look, to be honest, I don't either but right now he's one of our best options and," Frank says looking back at Zach, "He doesn't have a lot of options right now either."

"Hey Brother… seriously, I'm here to help." Zach says as he pushes his way through the Tsiatko. "I know I'm not looking good in your eyes right now but like he said, what choice do I have. I can't go back to the Committee as I'm a dead man if I do and I'm sure they're already hunting for me, so if I want to stay alive it's with you guys or nothing."

Frank looks to Brother and waits for his decision.

"You can have your time with him. I am not agreeing to let him go. Once you two have talked we will see where and how we move forward." Brother says.

"Thank you Brother, I will do right by you." Frank says. "Zach, let's go."

"Later guys." Zach says, smiling and saluting to his Tsiatko guards as he chases after Frank. Zach comes up close behind Frank and whispers. "Ok Frank, what was in the pouch? There's nothing sentimental about you?"

Frank peeks back at Zach. "Absolutely nothing."

"Bullshit." Zach responds as he comes along side.

"Fine then, its bullshit. Now you want to want to have our chat or have me send you back to them?"

"I'm good," Zach says, slapping Frank's shoulder. "And… really, thanks. I don't know why you saved my ass but thanks."

"I saved your ass because you're my back-up plan." Frank says as he ducks into his tent. Zach follows. Frank opens his pack and draws out a cell phone.

"Shit Frank," Zach whispers, "What're you doing with that, they're traceable. We agreed none."

"Will you just shut the hell up?" Frank whispers back. "It's shut off and there's no SIM card plus we're too deep in the mountain for a signal and we now need it."

"For what?"

Frank gives him the look and Zach keeps quiet while Frank powers up the phone. He sits down and signals Zach to do the same. Frank whispers to Zach. "Look, the Tsiatko may be listening and I don't want them knowing anything right now. We'll take turns texting back and forth. We keep things short and sweet. It's hokey but it's all I could come up with."

"You're right, it's hokey." Zach answers smirking and Frank starts.

"dont trust tsiatko not sure what to do, suggestions"

"take orb get out"

Frank shakes his head at Zach and grabs the phone.

"stop fuckin round"

Zach mouths back. "Ok, ok."

Frank continues texting. "a plan, a real plan"

Zach thinks for a moment then texts, "teams will hunt for me at ranier, not stupid. we need weapons and rations"

Frank takes the phone, "i have in san francisco"

"too far, 12hrs I have resources in seattle but need a tsiatko" Zach messages.

"u nuts" Frank replies

"they have ways to get where we cant go they merge thru anything u saw"

"how move tsiatko to seattle"

"truck, committee not look 4 u, u get truck, me and tsiatko meet u, get what we need return here."

Frank takes the phone but doesn't know what to reply.

Zach takes it back. "we defenseless no good holed up here its a start- better idea"

"No." Franks says out loud as he reads. He wipes his hands over his face. He's tired; he stinks and needs to breathe some fresh air. He would actually look forward to getting out of this cave and back to civilization, regardless of the risks.

"I can't believe you'd want to come back here." Frank whispers, ignoring the phone.

"Now that we found the Orb, there's no way in hell I'm walking away from it." Zach whispers back.

"Alright, your idea is crazy but let's talk to Brother and see if he'll let you out of here."

They walk back to where Brother is waiting not realizing there're two Tsiatko behind them. Obviously Brother wasn't taking any chances.

"Brother," Frank says "We have a plan but we'll need one of your… people, to come with us. We need your special abilities plus this way you'll know my companion will not be unguarded."

Zach speaks up, "There'll be teams, not just one at a time that hunted for you, that'll be scouring this area for me. We need to get to a nearby city for weapons to protect ourselves and the Orb. I am not doubting your capabilities but they have technology that may be challenging, even for you."

"How do you plan to do this?" Brother asks Frank.

Before Frank can answer, Zach speaks up again. "The Committee doesn't know what Frank looks like and they believe him to be dead. We need to be guided to an exit point closer to the bottom of the mountain. From there, Frank's job is to locate a truck suitable for carrying one of your… whatever I should call them." Zach says pointing aimlessly to the Tsiatko behind Brother.

Frank pipes back in. "I know the local town of Ashford and I'm sure I'll find something suitable there. We'll set a time to meet me at the parking lot of the park here. From there we'll head to Seattle which is only seventy miles away and we should be back in a day, a couple at most."

"If you have faith in your comrade, "Brother says, "I will as well but I must warn you, the one I am sending will deal with your companion if his words and actions are not true. He will not be forgiving on this matter." Brother utters a few grunts and whistles, the message is passed on and shortly another Tsiatko enters. If they believed Brother was immense, this one seems to dwarf him in comparison. It stands ten feet tall and has to weigh fifteen hundred pounds.

"This is one of my most trusted. He will accompany you."

"Christ Frank," Zach whispers "Do they have trucks that big in Ashton?"

Frank shrugs but he's not going to argue, "Brother I must ask. My companion has spoke of some of the powers you possess. I've seen you walk into the cave walls and I don't question your abilities but are you able to carry things through them as well as my comrade's plan does require this?"

Brother nods to their appointed Tsiatko escort, who approaches Frank. Without warning he grabs Frank and rushes the cave wall. Frank yells as his body is pressed against the hard, cold stone expecting to be crushed but his body blends with the stone and he finds himself engulfed in the very material that these walls are comprised of. His howling continues as he's pushed through the very fabric of the mountain and exists back into the cavern, a few feet away from where he began. He's still hollering as the Tsiatko drops him on the cavern floor. There's a look of shock on Zach's face. The one that was holding Frank is actually smiling. "What the fuck was that!" Frank shouts as he jumps up, his eyes have involuntarily turned Tsiatko black. "I didn't mean me for Christ's sake…holy fuck! Jesus, couldn't you have used my…I don't know…something, anything but me! Used that son of a bitch you say you don't trust?!" pointing to Zach. Frank takes a few steps, hands on his hips, taking deep breaths to calm down. "What would've happened if you'd let go of me?" Frank asks.

The Tsiatko looks to Brother to answer the question.

"You would have been crushed." Brother says. "As if the very mountain itself had dropped upon you."

Frank touches his body, patting himself down from head to toe as he walks in a circle. "Mother!"

Zach is stifling a laugh.

"Do you believe now?" Brother asks.

"Believe?" Frank says as he walks to the one who transported him through the wall. He points up to him, "Don't you ever, ever to that again…unless I ask you to or…it's really needed…ok?" Through panting breaths.

"As you wish my brother." The Tsiatko says looking into Frank's dark sockets, clamping his large hand on Frank's shoulder and nodding in agreement.

Frank's heart is still racing and his breathing is still heavy . He can't believe what he's just experienced, that was…very cool! "Ok, ok…I'm sold. I'd ask about the rest of your…capabilities but right now, I really don't want to know." He says. Frank checks his watch, it's almost one p.m., he thinks. He asks Brother to be sure. "Is it day or night?"

"It is day."

"Zach … we've got time, we can make it yet … c'mon, let's pack what we need."

Once they leave, Brother gives more specific instructions to their escort in their native tongue. Had Frank and Zach understand, it would have translated to "Whatever you do, you must protect our brethren Frank. His safety is critical to our survival here but he must not know of this or that this is your true mission. Keep him safe as best you can and if you must, let the other one die, he is nothing to us, just another means to achieve our goal. Take the utmost care of him and you and return to us safe and well."

"As you say." The escort replies.

CHAPTER TWO

"Have we made contact with Allmass yet?" Felix asks.

"No sir, not yet." Is the quick reply from his new personal assistant.

"What's your name again?" He asks even though the young man has been with him for a week already.

"Bertram sir." His assistant answers.

"What?" Felix asks.

"Bertram ... sir." He replies.

He can't keep their names straight and it has nothing to do with his age or mind. It's because they keep rotating new ones in every month now, for security reasons. They're all vetted but nothing is left to chance. Plus Bertram's looks throw Felix off. The lad is slim with black hair and bespectacled, always wearing tweed three piece suits with a bow tie. He's an adult twin to Harry Potter; he doesn't look like a Bertram to Felix. That's Felix excuse at least. He's eighty-five and he's being pressured to slow down and start letting go of the reins but he feels neither him nor the Committee can take the risk. There's too much at stake and they're so close.

"Alright then, leave me be, hold all calls and cancel any meetings I have. I need some privacy."

"Yes Mr. Belette. Do you want me to bring you anything to eat, it's getting late in the morning and you know what your doc..." Bertram stops mid-sentence seeing the look on his boss's face and immediately leaves, closing the double hand-made mahogany doors behind him.

Felix Belette walks over to an immense hand carved cherry wood cabinet that takes up only a fraction of the space in his private office. It has a built in bar hidden away in a pull out drawer. He pours two fingers of scotch and throws in a couple of ice cubes. His doctor is always telling him to avoid alcohol as it may mess with his prescriptions but as far as he's concerned, his doctor is full of shit. Felix is going partake in all the little things he likes as he ages, not regress to a bland healthy lifestyle that brings him no joy. He turns with drink in hand to survey his office. It's massive with dark paneled walls and matching hardwood floors. By the entrance doors is a large Balmoral tufted brown leather couch flanked by a Regency period handcrafted lazy chair, both placed on an elaborate Tabriz Persian rug, known for their fine bright wool weaves, elaborate colours and traditional patterns. The walls are filled with various stolen pieces of art that have been lost in time. The Portrait of a Young Man by Raphael, The Portrait of Adele as well as The Portrait of a Lady by Klimt, The Concert by Vermeer, The Storm on the Sea by Rembrandt and several others. He doesn't worry about publicly displaying these masterpieces as none of his guests that enter this sanctuary of his, would dare to reveal their existence or their location. There's not much else for adornment, nothing of a personal nature. He heads to his Theodore Alexander Mahogany desk with its alligator skin top and parks himself into his custom made dark brown, leather office chair. He swivels around to enjoy the view of his lush landscaped manor with the scenic mountains in the background, through floor to ceiling paned windows. He takes a sip, life is good. Felix believes he's a visionary with unique talents. He's sly and ruthless and has always been able to manipulate people, draw out information without most even realizing it. He's not charming; he has a foreboding presence that causes most to…spill their guts, so to say, as if they have a need to confess to him. The fear he induces has nothing to do with his size. He's nothing like his good old dad who was an imposing man, a general. His dad was six foot two, two hundred and fifty pounds of military might who had the respect of all under his command. Felix on the other hand is short with a small head, pointed nose, buck teeth with a long thin torso with short arms and legs. He's respected by few, feared by most. Loathed would be a better description. In his early days he had earned the nickname Weasel but back then, none would dare say it to his face, only behind his back or muttered under their breath. The Committee saw his potential, too bad his dad didn't, and so the general paid the price for not recognizing Felix for who and what he is…him and his precious aide, Captain William Dennison. He wished he'd have had a shot at that damn

Mr. H his father had so much faith in. He still celebrates the anniversary of that day he made the general and his aide pay the price. So many years ago, decades but it seems like yesterday to him. It was March twentieth, nineteen-fifty-three and he still revels in the memories of the conversation he had with his "dad" the day before, although he was never allowed to call him that in public. It had to be General Reeseman, yes sir… absolutely sir. Fuck you sir!

On that day, Felix knocked on the general's office door before entering, another rule. He's been summoned via good old Captain Bill. Captain Dennison opened the door, not saying a word but if looks could kill. Felix returned the look with a salute and a smile. Felix knew why he was here and yet, his dad didn't even give him the respect of berating him in person. He plunked down in the chair across the desk from the general and Bill took a place by the door, electing to remain standing.

"What's up?" Felix asks.

His dad's normal calm demeanor developed from years on the battlefield and in command is gone. His face is red and he looks like he's ready to explode. "Wipe that smirk off your face or I'm going to wipe it off for you. What the hell have you done?! Do you understand that you put the entire complex at risk with your actions… and what in the Sam Hill made you think what you did was ok? I just don't understand it… what were you thinking?!" The general barks out.

Felix looks back at Captain Dennison, back at his dad and chuckles. "Christ Pop, I was doing your job."

The general clenches his fists and pounds them on his desk. "What the blazes do you mean doing my job?! You just blew up a lab with a grenade, killed two of my scientists… you could have blown up this entire facility and you sit there laughing about it saying you're doing my job?!"

"Uh, yeah." Is Felix's reply, shaking his head giggling.

"There's something wrong with your mind! You were given a lot of responsibility. I really had to talk our civilian partners into letting you in and this is how you reward me… reward them by killing people?! God knows I have tried with you but no more. I'm not covering this kind of bullshit up for you. There's no getting out of this for you. I've given all I can but you have to be held accountable."

"Dad," Felix says giggling, "How fucking naive are you? I did what the Committee directed me to do. Something they knew you wouldn't have the balls for."

The general rises up from his chair, his arms reaching out ready to strangle Felix. "You son of a bitch, where do you get off making those comments?"

"Sit the hell down, old man! If you make one more move toward me, you and your lap dog Dennison will never see the light of day! The Committee will see to that!"

Captain Bill takes a step toward Felix but the general waves him off.

"Who the hell gave you the authority to speak for them and…they don't run things here, I do." The general says.

Felix looks back at Captain Dennison again, grins before turning back to the general. "What was it you said to Mr. H that day he first came on board…the military is a very big machine that requires a lot of grease?"

The general gives Bill an astonished look and brings his gaze back to Felix, "How the hell do you know what I said that day?"

"Oh, don't worry Pop, it wasn't your precious Captain. There are eyes and ears everywhere here. To use your own words…I work for the grease and it's the grease that runs things here. Man, you gotta take those blinders off." Felix says with another shake of his head. "You actually have no idea what the Solomons were doing in there, do you?"

The general gives Felix a blank look; not sure how to respond.

Felix sees this. "Exactly…that's my point, the Committee's point. The Solomon's were undermining everything and I'm sure your pet Mr. H had a hand in it as well and the two of you…didn't have a clue."

"Hang on there, boy, don't you go trying to discredit Horatio. He's put his life and soul into this program. If, and I mean if, the Solomons were doing anything improper…I know Mr. H had no knowledge of it. And, if the Solomons were up to no good, who are you or the Committee to just go and blow things up? Christ son doesn't the risk and ramifications involved with your actions mean anything? All the lives here you jeopardized?"

"Boy? Son? Where are those words coming from? You haven't called me those in at least a decade. I don't know what your game plan is but it's too late for that kind of back pedaling." Felix extracts a letter from his inside jacket pocket and slides it across the desk to the general.

"What's this?" The general asks.

"Read it for yourself."

His dad opens it and skims through the letter. "What kind of bullshit is this?" He asks, nodding to Captain Dennison to come over. The general hands it to him to read.

"No bullshit, like I told you, the grease is taking over. They've arranged seats for you on the plane leaving Roswell tomorrow that's transporting the re-assigned scientists to Oakland. You and Dennison are meeting with the president of Boeing, one of your civilian partners as you describe them. They have things to discuss." Felix says.

"You or anyone else is not telling me what to do on my own base." The general replies.

Felix gets up from his chair. "We'll see. You'll be receiving a call in about an hour, I suggest you take it. You've permitted your precious team to pull the wool over your eyes and I had to step in and clean up the mess. You're an embarrassment to me and to the Committee." With that, Felix turns his back on his dad and leaves.

The following afternoon, Felix is tracked down in the complex by a representative of the Committee who's just arrived.

"Mr. Reeseman, I regret to inform you that the plane transporting your father has mysteriously crashed. Unfortunately all thirty-five people on board have perished. Please accept our condolences. The Committee wanted me to inform you of this in person and also to formally request you assume the responsibilities of overseeing their interests in the Roswell project."

Felix smiles at the news. "My, my, such a tragedy…you never know how long you have in this world do you?" He's not looking for or expecting a response. "Thank the Committee for their condolences and their faith in me to carry matters through. Assure them they'll not be disappointed…again."

"Yes sir, I will."

Felix walks away but had anyone continued watching him, they'd have seen him give a skip and a jump a few yards down the hall. Felix did continue to prove his worth to the Committee and events such as the lab explosion, the plane crash and ultimately the fire that killed Mr. H were attributed to him whether he was directly involved or not. He continued to establish his voracity for violence, his reputation as the Weasel and his credibility to the Committee of getting the job done, regardless of the obstacles. The Committee appreciated his dedication so much so that when the Roswell Revelation project was shut down, he was promoted to the position of Appointed Representative, the AR for the Committee here in North America. With that appointment, he decided to change his last name to Belette, French for weasel. He was proud of his reputation and had grown accustomed to the reference and decided he wanted no further association with his father. To him, the name Reeseman was one to be ashamed of.

Felix's thoughts are interrupted by the entry of Bertram. He takes another sip of scotch as he swivels back around. "What?!" he shouts.

"Sir, you wanted me to advise you when the five Team Leaders would be available for your conference call." Bertram says.

The Team Leaders, ten in all, each command an elite unit assigned the task of tracking and eliminating the Tsiatko. These units were first created in the nineteen fifties and have been performing these clandestine operations ever since. Until now, Zachariah Allmass was in charge of these specialized teams.

"Oh, yes, of course. Give me a few minutes." Felix states. He doesn't like to communicate through email, text or any other written form, only through proven secure phone lines.

"Yes sir, I'll inform them." Bertram says leaving.

That son of a bitch Allmass, no better than that Mr. H. Felix knew…he knew Mr. H. was double crossing them in Roswell but he couldn't prove a damn thing and the Committee wouldn't let him touch him. When Horatio died in that fire, he thought his gut had steered him wrong but when Allmass came up with the evidence it was Mr. H after all who, not only stole the Orb but turned it over to the Tsiatko, he was kicking himself in the ass. And now Allmass is doing the same thing to him and he's going to pay for that. No one is going to make a fool of him. He knows Allmass wants the Orb for himself and it doesn't take a genius to figure out where he is, at Mt. Rainier. Him and his bullshit story, telling his office he'd be out of communication working with the teams and then telling his teams he'd be incommunicado with the Committee. Coercing everyone into thinking the Tsiatko moved the Orb south. Felix picks up the phone "Everyone there?"

There's a resounding unified reply of "Yes sir."

Felix is smart enough to know not to use all his resources on the task he's about to send these men on so only half of the teams will be deployed. "Ok, here's how things stand. Allmass has gone rogue and wants the Orb for himself. We know the Tsiatko have the Orb and I'm sure they're holed up at Mt. Rainier with it probably along with Allmass. Allmass was feeding us false intelligence when he sent everyone south. You guys know the drill. You forget about him being your boss! I want your teams dispatched to Rainier but keep things low key. You find this mother fucker and you bring him to me, alive! I expect results. But I want to make it clear it's Allmass that's the primary target. If you have an opportunity at the Orb, take it but that target is secondary." With that he hangs up. Felix knows Allmass has shared little with him or the Committee of what he all knows about the Tsiatko or the Orb and, he was okay with that as long as Zach got the job done. Now, it's a different story. Felix is going to take great pleasure in personally extracting every shred of information he can from Allmass. It's going to be a slow and agonizing process for Zachariah and Felix is going to savor every minute of it.

CHAPTER THREE

There's little for Frank and Zach to pack, most everything is staying behind. They take the one clean change of clothes they have left, water and a few rations. They throw on their PVC suits, clip on gas monitors, headlamps and are good to go. Brother and their escort are waiting for them.

"We're ready." Frank says.

"You will be taken to a place that is a short distance from where you requested. From there, it is up to you. I wish you luck." Brother says.

"What do we call you?" Franks asks, referring to their escort.

"It is a name spoken in our tongue, one which you would not understand or mimic." He replies.

"Give it a try and we'll see." Frank says.

It utters a short, rolling sound grunt followed by a quick whistle combined with a growl.

"Seriously?" Zach asks.

"As I have told you." He says.

"No offense but how about you let us come up with a name we can work with, like Brother has done with the name he chose for us to use?" Frank asks.

He looks at Brother for approval, who nods in agreement.

"Yes." He says.

"Ok." Frank says and looks at Zach.

"I don't know." Zach says "Why're you looking at me?"

"For fu…we'll come up with something." Frank states.

As they're led past the cavern area holding the Orb, Frank and Zach switch on their headlamps and they continue on through the seemingly unending labyrinth within Mt. Rainier. They've no idea what direction they're heading. They trod along for an hour before they see a distant light ahead. As they near, they can see it's an opening but it's blocked with an array of large fallen trees, roots and several small boulders. They stop at the entranceway, drop their packs and get out of their PVC suits, tossing them in a corner along with their headlamps.

"Wait." Says their escort as he penetrates through all the debris. It's one thing to see them walk into the walls but to witness a Tsiatko blend into the very material it's passing through is amazing. As his body moves through the trees, roots and rocks, it assumes the composite of each it intermixes with. Its head, body and limbs becoming one with each piece as it encounters it. One second his head is part timber while his arm or leg becomes a branch, with another stride his leg is partially stone and a foot becomes a tree root as various other body parts remain Tsiatko. He's engulfed in it all and then disappears from sight. Moments later he re-emerges, his body going through the same process with his return. Frank knows, no matter many times he may witness this, he'll always be blown away by this spectacle.

"Just think Frank … that was you earlier." Zach chuckles.

The Tsiatko looks at Frank "It is safe, shall I carry you through?"

"Uh … no, as much as I enjoyed it last time, I'll pass. Anyway we can make an opening for us to crawl through?"

"Yes." The Tsiatko says looking back at the entranceway. He passes back through to the exterior and they can hear him working from the outside.

They do what they can from the inside and in a short time, there's a large enough space for them to exit and Frank and Zach struggle their way through. It's about mid-day and they can see, through a break in the trees, that they're overlooking the parking area and the ranger's office. They're at the base of a bluff similar to the location where Mr. H's body was found. Their escort is not in sight but steps out from the cliff wall as they're scanning for him.

"For fuck sakes!" Zach gasps, glaring at him. Their guide has a puzzled look.

"Zach … Zach." Frank calls again before he gets his attention. "One way or another, you're gonna have to get used to it. I'm heading down to see if I can catch a ride to Ashford, otherwise I'll walk or hitchhike, its only six miles. When it gets dark, you two make your way down and I'll be watching for you."

"And what if you don't come up with something?" Zach asks.

"Just leave that to me, I'll find something even if I have to steal it." Frank replies. He heads out, reminding himself that he won't be recognized as he looks nothing like the he did when he once patrolled this area as a Deputy Sherriff. Thinking about his looks, it hits him that he should visit the public washrooms before going to the Rangers' office. He hasn't seen himself in a mirror for awhile and, as he sniffs his shirt, he needs a wash before being around anyone else. Even though it's still winter, there's substantial traffic at the park even with the limited hiking trails open. There are snowmobilers, cross country skiers and those simply out to enjoy the views but thankfully that's where most must be as the bathroom is empty. He removes his shades and pulls off his floppy hat as he looks in the mirror, revealing his full head of brown and slightly silver hair now grown out to a burr cut hair style. He looks like shit. There're large purplish bags under his grey eyes and his full grey beard burying his cleft chin, is a tangled mess and almost down to his chest. He strips down to the waist revealing his tattooed upper body. He's glad he hasn't lost much muscle as he looks at the chiseled five ten, two hundred pound frame reflecting back at him. The rigorous trekking through the mountains and the caverns has more than compensated for the gym time he sorely misses. He may be sixty but he's still a little self-obsessed. He gives his beard a hand-soap shampoo, scrubs the rest of his face, gives himself a quick sponge bath and ends his preening by running his fingers through his beard trying to make himself as presentable as possible. Satisfied, he leaves and enters the ranger's office pretending to look at the assorted park brochures, eavesdropping for any conversations of those that may be heading to Ashford. He'd walk but would rather not. He's wanders about for twenty minutes before a familiar face walks in and beelines it to the office's main information desk. It's Oin, the stoner who first found Mr. H's remains.

"Thanks, dude." Oin says dropping off a wrench and heads back for the door.

Frank follows him out, letting him get a hundred feet away from the office before he approaches him.

"Hey, Oin… wait up!" He calls

Oin looks back. He can't place this guy who's called out to him. "Ah… no entiendo ingles senor." He says and continues on his way.

Frank smiles and runs up to him. "Oin… it's me Deputy Smirnov, the guy you and Willow talked to when you found the body here." He whispers loudly.

Oin hesitates and stares at Frank. "Dude…Deputy Dan? Is that you? Hey man…never would've recognized you. What's with the look and the civvies? And whoa…you're ripe man…you need a wash or something…man, that's nasty."

Frank ignores his comments. "Look, call me Frank." As he gently grabs Oin's elbow, leading him farther away and stops in the parking lot. "I need your help."

"Hey man…you did righteous by me and Willow…like sure…what can I do man?"

"Look, I need a ride into Ashford but you can't tell anyone you saw me, know me or what I look like."

Oin scans around, "Really man…you like undercover or something? Did it have to do with that body…I mean like, yea…I'm into this man…I dig this cloak and dagger stuff."

"I'm going to trust you Oin. I am undercover and I need someone I can trust. Can I trust you?"

"Dude, I mean Frank…I'm with you?" Oin replies excitedly. He suddenly slouches like he's trying to hide even though he's out in the open.

Oin is still a little over the top but not nearly as intense as their first meet. Frank pulls him back upright. "You have a car?" He asks.

"Really? Man…I have a car!" Oin says beaming and leads Frank towards a far corner of the lot.

As they progress, Frank sees they're heading toward an old nineteen fifties era International Metro Van. These were used commercially as delivering vehicles back in their day, quite often as bread and milk trucks. This one's been converted to a Hot Rod step van. "Are you kidding me?" Franks asks in amazement. "This is yours?"

Oin smiles. "Yea…awesome isn't it? When my granddad passed a couple years back, he left me a few bucks so Willow and I put it into this."

"Where is Willow?" Silent Willow, Frank named her as she hardly uttered a word.

"Oh…she's visiting her mom so I thought I'd head out on my own for a few days."

Frank 's impressed as he tours around it. It has its original patina which is a blend of faded white and rust colour and he can still make out the faint image of the original "Bob's Dry Cleaning" lettering. The chrome grill has been re-done along with the triple diamond front emblem; it has eighteen inch wheels, double entry rear doors and the typical slide doors on the front passenger and driver's side. Oin is beaming as he slides open the passenger door and steps in. Frank follows and sees a Cadillac Denali seat has replaced the original driver's seat and it looks like a custom leather driving wheel was installed in lieu of the factory large diameter one.

"Sweet, isn't it?" Oin asks. "This baby has a total off frame restoration with a reinforced chassis, a GMC S-15 front suspension, two inch Bell spindles and front disc brakes. The rear suspension is from a seventy C-10 with a RideTech air suspension, I dropped a 5.3L Vortec V8 into this ride with a four speed auto tranny to a Chevy rear end." Oin sounds like he knows what he's talking about.

Frank steps into the seven foot long cargo area, where the smell of marijuana still lingers, and stops beside a black leather bench seat Oin has installed against one wall. Frank can nearly stand fully upright.

"I have reinforced hardwood floors and, this," as he pats the backrest of the bench, "Folds down to a bed when we need it. And plenty of room for my gear." As he points to the two duffle bags stowed near the bench. "This machine can haul seven thousand pounds."

Frank pulls off his pack and takes a seat beside Oin. "This," as he inspects the interior once more, "Is fucking outstanding … it's perfect."

Oin bobs his head. "Cool dude … I'm glad you like. So when you want to get rockin into Ashford?"

CHAPTER FOUR

Zach sits uncomfortably with the Tsiatko in the cave waiting for Frank's return. It's been a couple hours. He's been quietly watching his Tsiatko guard who, in turn, is watching him in silence.

"You don't give me the same looks as the other Tsiatko do?" He finally says.

"I do not understand."

"The others act like they're ready to rip me apart, hate in their eyes, which is understandable for what I have done but ... you don't seem to look at me that way."

"I have been taught that it is not my place to judge ones as insignificant to the greater good as you humans are. It would be like you judging the ants that scatter at your feet as you walk this earth." Is the Tsiatko's unemotional reply.

"Really?" Zach asks sarcastically.

"Yes."

"I'm ... I'm not really sure what to say to that. Ants you say? Interesting, yep, just an hour or two to go ... the excitement is going to kill me."

Before Zach can comment further, Frank calls out to them. "I'm coming in!"

"Why are you back? Are they looking for me already?" Zach asks as Frank enters.

"No, no, all is good. I found a vehicle already." Frank answers.

"Seriously? How?" Zach asks.

"I bumped into somebody from my past and he's willing to let us use his but there's a hitch ... he's coming with us." Before Zach can say another word, Frank yells out "Oin, get in here!"

"Are you crazy?" Zach murmurs as Oin makes his way in. "We have a goddamn Tsiatko with us."

"Don't worry." Frank says smiling as Oin appears. "I trust him and he's a stoner, no one's going to believe him if shit hits the fan." He whispers.

"What?!" Zach replies.

"Oin, I have some friends I want you to meet, they're helping me out too."

Oin stands. It's taking a moment for his eyes to adjust. "Cool. This is a bitchin cave. How far in does it go? I've done some exploring here but never came across anything like this man. Whoa…ripe in here too dude. Sorry, I mean Frank. That's potent stuff."

"Oin, this is Zach, short for Zachariah. Zach, Oin."

"Cool dude." Oin says as he gives Zach a fist bump gesture.

Zach hesitates but then extends his for a fist bump greeting. "Yea…good to meet you too Oin." Zach says.

"Zach…Z-man, yea that's a cool name for you. Frank and Z-man. Hey…it's coming to me man. Franknzee. Yea, like a monster ready to set its wrath on the world. Franknzee takin on the bad guys. Yea…I dig it." Oin says.

Frank chuckles. He can't help it. He's getting déjà vu from his first meet with Oin. "Oin…Oin? Hey as much as I like the sound of that, how about we stick with Frank and Zach." Frank says.

"Ok, ok, I'm cool with that." He replies.

Zach is dumbfounded.

"And," Frank says "This is another…associate of mine." As he points to the figure standing in the semi-dark corner near the entrance.

The Tsiatko steps out towards Oin.

Oin is silent as he takes a couple steps back and looks up, way up. He grabs onto Frank's shoulder with both hands, almost for support. There's a look of shock on his face. "Whoa, " As he moves toward the Tsiatko. "Tell me I'm trippin. You're hangin with a Bigfoot! How rad is that!"

"They're actually called See-at-ko." Franks says.

"See-at-ko." Oin repeats slowly extending his fist toward it. The Tsiatko is unsure how to respond but slowly puts out his, as he had seen Zach do and fist bumps. The Tsiatko's clenched hand is at least ten times larger than Oin's.

Oin laughs. "No fucking way. What's your name dude?"

The Tsiatko states his name in his native tongue.

"What is that?" Oin asks.

"My name." The Tsiatko answers.

"Dude…you can speak?" Oin laughs. "This is whack, man. But seriously… you gotta come up with a better name if we're gonna work together." He turns to Frank. "Right?"

Before Frank can answer, Zach interrupts, "Frank, can I talk to you privately for a minute? Excuse us guys." As he walks a little farther into the cave, indicating to Frank to follow.

"Look, you two…uh, chat and we'll just be a minute." Frank says smiling and walks back to Zach.

"What the fuck did you tell him?" Zach whispers.

"I just gave him a quick story about how we're undercover on a secret mission to save the world, battling bad guys and that we have to go to Seattle to smuggle out weapons we need to fight with. That's about it." Frank says, chuckling as he looks back at the other two. He can hear their conversation.

"So like…I gotta ask, do you mind if I touch your fur?" Oin asks the Tsiatko.

The Tsiatko seems uncomfortable with the question, looking over at a grinning Frank. "Uh, okay." He answers.

"Frank? What were you doing, telling him that?" Zach asks.

"Look," Frank says as he returns his attention to Zach, "Oin's harmless and I figured why not, I had nothing to lose because he wasn't giving up his vehicle no matter what."

"Wow, this is really soft man. It smells but it's not what I expected." Oin comments as he walks behind the Tsiatko. The Tsiatko turns following Oin's movements.

"So what did you expect to happen when he saw the Tsiatko" Zach asks.

"This." Frank says as he continues listening at Zach but is intently watching the other two. He finds the interaction between them almost hypnotic.

The Tsiatko makes a circle as Oin walks around him.

"How tall are you man? You gotta weigh over a ton? What do you eat?" Oin asks bombarding him with questions.

"I…I don't know," replies the Tsiatko clearly confused by Oin's attitude towards him and his on-going questioning. "I eat vegetables, fruit, roots, that kind of things."

"Frank?" Zach says tugging at Frank's arm to get him to face him. "How do you know him?"

"You know my girlfriend Willow; well she's not here right now she's visiting her mom you know. Her mom's not feeling too good…so I came here solo, but anyways she's a hairdresser you know…been doing it for awhile. So…she could do something righteous and funky for you…yea dude, made you look bad ass." Oin says.

"Willow? I do not know hairdresser." The Tsiatko answers.

"Him and his girlfriend are the ones that found Mr. H which led me to the cache and the castle." Franks says to Zach. Frank can't picture Silent Willow as a stylist, not that she said much but something about her suggested her role in life would have been something more substantial.

Zach has an appalled look on his face. "You're fucking with me aren't you?"

"Willow is my girlfriend dude, you know…my partner." Oin says to the Tsiatko.

The Tsiatko nods his understanding.

"And a hairdresser is one that cuts and styles hair, man." Oin pulls off his toque to display his. "She cuts mine all the time. She could really do something wild with you. Man…I wish she was her…she'd be freakin. She'd have all the other Tsiatko babes on you like glue after she was done." Oin laughs.

"No, I'm not." Frank answers to Zach's question.

"What…and it's just a coincidence that he's here now? You don't think that's a bit odd?"

Zach asks.

"No, he hangs here all the time, likes to get one with nature." Frank says as he turns back to the other two. He's being entertained by the interaction between them. In awe of it actually.

"Babes, I do not understand babes." The Tsiatko says.

"You know…women, the other sex." Oin remarks as he gives the Tsiatko a wink and a smile. "Girlfriend? Mate? You know what I mean dude." As he gives the Tsiatko a nudge. "You have a mate?"

"Uh, no…no mate." It replies.

"Sad man. Dude…you gotta have someone to share your life with." Oin says. "Another soul to travel through time with. Going solo doesn't do you any good.

Listen…you need some tips man? I can help. I did alright in my day. Seriously man, you gotta trust me on this."

"Thank you, I will keep that in mind." The Tsiatko says nodding his head, clearly uneasy with this discussion.

Frank turns to Zach. "Look…we go with Oin and take our chances." He says "That's the way it is. We have no more time to waste. Just accept it." He walks back to the other two with Zach reluctantly following.

"Ok," Frank says, "This is how we're going to play this. You," Indicating the Tsiatko, "I need you to wait here until its dark while the three of us make our way to the parking lot down there and place Oin's van in a spot where you won't be seen when you get there."

"I cannot." Interrupts the Tsiatko, "I am not letting him," nodding to Zach, "out of my sight. That is my orders. I will not permit this. I have sworn."

Frank rubs his face and gives a tug on his beard. "Ok, Oin and I will head down now. You too follow later and we'll be waiting. Zach, it's an old fifty-three International van, the kind they used as delivery trucks. You know the kind I mean?" Frank asks Zach.

"Yea, I know." Zach replies.

"Oin and I will park it so the rear end is against the back of the lot, out of view. Frank says. He looks to the Tsiatko, "It has double back doors so you should be able to squeeze in. It's might be a snug fit but you should be comfortable."

It nods its acknowledgement.

"Alright, let's go." Frank says.

"High fives dudes!" Oin yells out as he raises his hand. "Rock on!"

"Uh, no." Frank says and crawls out.

"OK." Oin says a rejected look on his face. "Later," He adds as he follows Frank.

CHAPTER FIVE

Brother looks like a hairy version of the Thinker as he sits poised on a rock staring at the Orb on top of the crystallized boulder. He's been watching it for hours. After Frank and Zach's departure, he's placed a small circle of stones around it to ensure it does not move or is accidently touched since he permitted Frank to take the pouch used to transport here. The same pouch Mr. H had presented it to the Tsiatko, as a gift towards their salvation. How right but how wrong he was with his actions. For the Tsiatko, any direct contact with it is lethal, catastrophic and cataclysmic for them, this planet and all life it holds. This was the end result on their ancestor's previous home, Mars as these humans call it. That's how the Handlers designed it.

On Mars, the Tsiatko's forefathers thought they had won, finally ridding their home of these… pests who had over run their world back then, the same as they have now on this planet. But no, they had lost once more. This is the truth and the reality of it all, as it was passed down through the ages by folklore from their original ancestors. The Tsiatko are the last branch of their kind. They do not have the capabilities of relocating to other worlds as their predecessors once did. Although the Tsiatko are considered mystical Beings with powers humans cannot comprehend, they are but a remnant of what their forefathers were; the result of interbreeding with the Neanderthals. This planet is their last stronghold. The only place left that they can call home.

Frank was so right in his words as to the lengths humans will go to protect what they believe is theirs and the weaponry they will use. To Brother, it was only a moment in time ago that man chose to try and eliminate a portion of them by using an explosive device on Mt. St. Helens. They felt the impact of the explosion here at Rainier and the devastation to their numbers was substantial. They lost so many, including many elders that had roamed this planet for eons and so Brother had to take the place of those that were lost. His heart still feels the loss, the sorrow and the pain. His taste for revenge is still strong, and with Frank's unknowing participation, Brother will have his vengeance and reclaim what is rightfully theirs.

CHAPTER SIX

They've been on the road for close to an hour now since leaving Mt. Rainier in Oin's van. Frank is driving and Zach has a seat on the padded front cover encasing the engine. Zach is turned sideways, watching what scenery he can out the passenger window. Frank is concentrating on the road. They haven't said a word to each other since they left the park. The Tsiatko is sitting on the floor in a sitting position with his back against the rear doors, his arms folded across his chest and his feet towards the front. If this is his first time traveling in any type of vehicle and having difficulty with it, he's not showing it. Oin is sprawled out on the bench seat still going on with endless stories to his Tsiatko traveling companion who's simply listening. They're nearing Alma on the way to Seattle and Frank spots a full service truck stop featuring a restaurant, showers and a host of other amenities.

"Zach," Frank says "I don't know about you but I could use a shower, a change of clothes and some real food, you?"

"Definitely, you needn't ask."

Frank pulls in and parks in the darkest corner of the lot he can find. He turns to the Tsiatko. "Look, I understand you swore an oath to watch Zach but we both need to clean up and food, we can't function without it. So I need you to trust me with him. I'm going to leave Oin here with you along with the keys for the van. You must understand we NEED both you and this van, so we have to come back."

The three of them wait for the Tsiatko's answer as it contemplates Frank's proposal. "I agree to your terms." It answers. It's feeling a fellowship with Oin and is actually enjoying his company.

"Bitchin." Oin smiles and says. "You bros take your time. Me and … my pal here are just gonna chill."

"Remember Oin, STAY in the van, got it?" Frank emphasizes as he tosses Oin the keys.

"I got it Frank." Oin assures him.

"You want us to grab you two anything, something to eat or drink?" Frank clarifies for the Tsiatko.

The Tsiatko nods no and Oin replies "No, I'm good. I've got a few things in my bag if the big dude changes his mind."

Frank and Zach head in and Zach does a double take as he passes the mirrors in the shower room. He throws his bag on the floor and leans into the mirror propping himself on the counter as he closely examines his image. Frank may be a bit self-obsessed but Zach is downright vain. "Holy shit!" Zach exclaims.

"Don't worry pretty boy. It's only temporary." Frank says laughing as he continues on to a shower stall.

Zach yanks off his headwear. His long slicked back black hair is a greasy mess. "Gross." He says tossing his hat in the garbage can. His dark tan is fading and his square chin and high cheekbones are concealed by thick dark facial hair. There're large ugly bags hanging under his sky blue eyes from lack of sleep and he's developing a unibrow. He strips down in front of the mirror, not caring who may enter and witness his actions. He's the same height as Frank but a leaner version weighing in at one hundred and eighty pounds. His metrosexual manicured body has hair sprouting everywhere. "For fucks sake," He says shaking his head at all the past effort gone to waste.

"Will you hurry up? We don't have the time." Frank yells from his stall.

"Yea, yea," Zach replies gathering up his things.

They know they should hurry but they take their time as the hot shower feels so good. They decide hell with it and sit to enjoy a meal of steak and eggs along with an endless stream of coffee. They're beginning to feel human again after spending so many days in such an alien environment.

"I guess we should, before Oin drives our friend crazy." Frank says chuckling.

"Yea, I guess so." Zach reluctantly agrees.

The van is still in its isolated spot but as they slide open the doors, a smoky haze floats out of the van combined with the definite aroma of weed. They wait a few moments before entering to allow the smoke in the cab to clear. They get in and witness the Tsiatko sitting cross legged on the floor facing the bench where

Oin is seated. There's a bong on the floor between them along with a couple open bags of chips and a big bag of what was gummy bears. The Tsiatko slowly turns to face them, there's no hiding the glazed look in his eyes and he smiles a wide toothy grin.

"Franknzee…you guys are back. Oin blurts out. "Me and Gaylord have been getting acquainted and I've been teaching him a few of our customs."

The Tsiatko gives a thumb up sign.

Frank and Zach look at each other. "Gaylord?" Zach asks chuckling. "Gaylord? And you're good with that?"

"Gaylord" gives another thumb up sign. Frank and Zach can't help but laugh.

'Hey…this is one regal dude, the name suits him man." Oin says solemnly as he gives Gaylord a pat on the shoulder.

"What're you doing getting him high? We need him at his best." Frank says.

"Listen man," Oin says. "This stuff has only a fifteen percent THC level and an eight percent CBD. It doesn't mess with your mind, just makes you…mellow. It's anti-anxiety, anti-inflammatory and an analgesic. Guys, with this, nothing…I mean nothing will get you hyped…you're gonna be calm no matter what. No negative vibes at all." Oin replies.

"What are you, a chemist or something?" Zach says.

"No dude… no chemist or scientist, I just know my stuff and this stuff is righteous. I'm not going to put just anything into my body Z." Oin says seriously. "So I decided that me and the big boy here just needed to chill out with my bong cause…like, his hands are just too big to hold a joint." Oin giggles and Gaylord joins in with a roaring laugh.

"No, it is good." Gaylord says once he stops laughing. "I have enjoyed participating in this custom."

"Custom?" Frank asks.

"Yes." Gaylord says. "Oin explained to me that this is a respected human ritual before going into battle and I did not want to offend my friend." As he gently slaps Oin on the knee. "I am honoured."

"Friend?" Zach says.

"Yes, my friend … and he has been teaching me the ways you humans communicate, Oorah!" Gaylord announces abruptly raising his fist in the air, accidently pounding the roof and leaving a substantial dent.

Frank grabs the bong. "Ok, no more for you two, that's it." And places it up front, out of their reach.

"I understand, my other friend." Gaylord says to Frank. "I am as prepared for war as I need to be. But I do now have a need for sustenance. How did you phrase it Oin? Oh, yes, I am feeling peckish and I need…" he looks to Oin and watches as Oin mouths the word for him, "Munchies." Gaylord exclaims smiling. Three zucchini, ten packages of alfalfa sprouts and six cans of nuts later Gaylord is good to go, catnapping in the back with Oin.

They've been back on the road a half hour. In another hour they should be at the location in Seattle that's their destination. Zach looks over at Frank and the bong that is now sitting between them.

"Oin did say it just makes you mellow… that nothing will get you hyped." Zach says.

Oin is careful not to stir and opens his eyes only slightly enough to watch Frank and Zach take a few hits. His role as a Handler playing Oin again was only to get the van into the hands of Frank, nothing more. But he couldn't resist actively aiding them and actually meeting a Tsiatko rather than intervening from a distance as he, Willow and Stogie Man have done for so many thousands of years. He's never been stoned before and it's taking longer to clear his head than he thought. He was to have met up with his fellow Handlers hours ago at a designated spot near Ashford but he was too wrapped up in what he was doing. He'll have to deal with the consequences later.

CHAPTER SEVEN

"Son of a bitch!" Felix yells as he throws his half full glass of scotch and ice across the room sending glass, liquor and ice flying. It's been gnawing at him…eating away at him ever since he made the decision to send those teams after Allmass. Something isn't adding up. Allmass is up to more than it appears. He kicks the metal garbage can near his desk, scattering debris everywhere.

Bertram bursts into his office. "Mr. Belette, is everything okay?"

"Does it look like everything's okay?" Felix shouts back. "Does this appear to be the actions of an individual who believes everything's okay?"

"I'm not sure sir. I haven't been here long enough."

The comment catches Felix off guard and he takes a moment to take a breath. "No…I guess you haven't. Get Reggie in here ASAP and send someone in here to clean up this mess."

"Yes sir."

Felix takes a seat behind his desk and wonders why he didn't see this before. Maybe he's getting to old for this crap. Bertram returns with another one of the hired help and they both take a couple minutes to get his office back to normal. Felix is calmer now. "Thank you." He says as they leave.

A few minutes later Reggie enters. Reggie is an attractive woman in her mid-forties. She's Irish with a tall, slender, long limbed physique, flowing red hair and piercing green-blue eyes upon a lightly freckled face of pale skin. She has a Masters in Psychology and Behavioral Sciences and was an analyst and profiler for the FBI before she was recruited by the Committee. She has a reputation for being extremely thorough and efficient. Reggie is her nickname, short for Rajeena, Rajeena Byrnes. As she told it, her dad wanted a boy and since she was the last of five girls, he gave her the nickname. She grew up to be a confident strong woman but being embedded in fields erroneously classified as a working man's world she elected to keep using it. Many a male counterpart is more than a bit surprised when they meet her in person.

"Mr. Belette, is everything alright? You look a bit tense. Bertram told me what happened. This isn't your normal behavior?"

"Quit it Reggie. I'm not in the mood."

"Why aren't you?"

Felix gives her an exasperated look. "Seriously, not now."

"Of course Mr. Belette." She says.

Reggie has a reputation for constantly analyzing people. The way they talk, look, body language, actions, it never stops with her and she has gotten under his skin so many times with it. That's why he likes her so much.

"You know Allmass? Zachariah Allmass?"

"I do."

"He's dropped off the radar. I know he's up to no good. I want you to go back through everything he's been involved with in the last six months. Anything and everything. What transactions he's approved, personnel, travel, contacts, I don't want any stone unturned. Especially his time in Washington State."

"What are you hoping to find?"

"I'm not telling you. I want to see what you find but look for it like you're looking for dirt. Understand me?"

"Of course. And when do you need this?"

"Yesterday. Nothing, I repeat nothing is more important to you than this. Am I clear on that?"

"Sir, you know me and my work." She replies cocking her head slightly.

"I do, sorry."

"Are you sure you wouldn't want talk about things a bit? It may do you some good." She asks smiling.

"Get out." He says with a smirk.

"Your loss." She says as she leaves.

"Oh…if I was only younger and taller," Felix thinks.

Thirty-six hours later she's sets up a meeting with Felix in the conference room. He walks in to see one of the tables hosts an assortment of juices, coffee, pastries and sandwiches. She's constantly munching while she works even though she tries to maintain a healthy and regular eating schedule. Reggie is pouring over a portable cork board that almost takes up an entire wall, where she's posted a variety of documents and pictures. More of the same are scattered across the main board room table. To the unknowing eye, it may look like a disorganized mess but Felix knows better.

"Mr. Belette, morning, something to eat or drink?"

"When are you going to start calling me Felix? And no, no appetite right now, thanks."

"Uh, never." She says with a wink. "There's quite an array of goodies there, you don't know what you're missing out on?"

Felix takes a chair. "So what have you got?"

"Well, it's nothing that stands out but little things that started with his communication style that has changed. It becomes more evident at the time he reported the find of Mr. H's caches, the castle and the deaths of his two agents along with a Deputy Sherriff named Frank Smirnov."

"Wasn't Smirnov identified as an anomaly, so that would make sense?"

"Yes but…look I'm not going to go through all the minute details but it's when you put all the small inconsistencies together, you get a better picture. It may be hard to follow as I may jump back and forth about things but I'll try and be clear as I can. If I lose you along the way, stop me. I do have a habit of thinking out loud as I go." She warns.

"Ok, show me what you've got."

"I started with Smirnov. Here we have a sixty year old guy working in law enforcement, who has no passport. Who is this day and age, living in the U.S., especially since 9/11 doesn't have a passport?"

"I'm not sure." is Felix's reply.

"What? Oh…sorry, this is me talking out loud with questions. Just bear with me."

"Okay, please proceed and I'll try and not to respond to everything."

"Ok, where was I? Smirnov…the guy had one account for payroll when he died, with not much in it and no credit cards yet, moving back in his life, he disappears off the grid regularly. What does he go and how does he live? His tax records show nothing for the times he disappears. I mean, I'm talking about a

Deputy Sherriff who earned fifty-five thousand a year but, according to the police report, had thousands of dollars worth of designer suits, a ton of art work and a high end collectible Mercedes. How is this possible?" Reggie moves to the food table and grabs a croissant, biting down on it as she returns to the board. "Now… as far back as any records go, he was raised by his grandparents in the Midwest but there's no birth certificate for him. They migrated to the U.S. before he was born so where did he come from?"

"What does that mean?" Felix asks.

Reggie doesn't hear his question. She's too engrossed in her thoughts. "And… why didn't Allmass," As she heads in another direction of her investigation, "Call you in on this castle find right away, the place your supposed dead Mr. H was living where Allmass discovered he gave the Orb to the Tsiatko? And how exactly did he know that? I mean, that's a major development. And why did he immediately torch everything? It makes no sense."

"I never thought of it that way." Felix responds.

"Yes, I know."

Felix isn't sure if that was a disparaging remark or simply a comment.

"So I decided to look into Allmass's background more. When Allmass was recruited, he elected to change his looks along with his name and he created Zachariah Allmass. I can understand this. People sometimes despise who there were and want a fresh start. Allmass must have really hated what he was because he went to the extreme. The man had issues. Sorry, me analyzing a bit but it helps."

"No, go ahead."

She points to a school enrollment record on the board, "Before that he was Adam Pope, Adam Zachariah Pope, and he went to the same small town school as Frank Smirnov only a year behind. In small town schools, everyone knows everybody." Reggie raises her eyebrows to Felix.

"You're kidding me?" He says.

Reggie sweeps a few flakes off your top and walks over to pour a black coffee, taking a couple sips as she makes her way back to the board. "Now I can understand Smirnov not recognizing Allmass because of the surgery but Allmass should have recognized him. I checked the school yearbooks against Smirnov's Sherriff's

I. D., there's a clear resemblance even after all these years. And, comments in the yearbooks suggest they and their families socialized to some degree."

"Son of a bitch." Felix remarks as he gets up and walks to the board.

"Okay, let's leave that for a minute." Reggie continues as she directs his attention to some other papers. "Here, through an off-shore account shortly after Smirnov was killed, Allmass paid for a group of mercenary contractors to take out a target in Belize. A guy named Roman Petrov rumoured to be a Russian assassin… supposedly to have done a ton of hits but nothing that can be confirmed. The mercs failed; all dead as reported by the Belize officials and no trace of Petrov. Just dead bodies stacked up in his house. Why did Allmass hire outside the firm and why take out this guy… and why no reports about it? He paid top dollar for this target and we have nothing on record. Does this name ring a bell with you?" She asks.

"Not at all." Felix says.

"Well, here is where it gets even more strange. Petrov's activities flair up every time Smirnov disappears. What would that indicate to you?"

"I'm not sure… unless, they're one and the same? But … how is that possible if Smirnov was dead before the contract on Petrov?" Felix asks.

"It's not." She smiles and pulls another report from the table. "I located the passport picture of Petrov, bearded and bald and ran it through facial recognition software against the clean cut Smirnov using his Sherriff's I.D. and … it's the same guy." She hands the report to Felix.

"Goddamn it, why didn't we catch any of this before?"

"Why would we? There was absolutely nothing to red flag things at this end. Smirnov had no passport so NSA or Border Security software wouldn't have caught it. It was only because of your instincts we got this far." Reggie says trying to throw Felix a compliment.

"Let me correct you." Felix says. "It's because of you and your talents that we got anywhere on this."

"Oh, you're so sweet." She replies giving him a pouty look as she sets her cup down and brushes the remaining bits of croissant off her hands before continuing. "And here is where it gets even weirder. Allmass was spending substantial time in San Francisco just before he disappeared right? According to his reports he wanted to investigate more where his team got wiped out, supposedly by the

Tsiatko. I checked the local newspapers and there was a big write up at the same time about a street gang member executed in an empty warehouse. It got a lot of attention as it was pretty gruesome, shot up from head to toe while tied down in a chair."

"Why would that catch your attention? What makes that so special?"

"The gang member was killed in the same warehouse that a few years before, members of the Italian mob were taken out. There are no suspects in either case but it was rumoured that the boss of the local Russian mob was responsible for the Italians."

"And?" Felix says.

"The gang member killed was one of the shooters that killed Petrov's girlfriend years before that had just ditched the Witness Protection Program he was in. When the Italians were killed, Petrov was the mob boss's personal driver. I suspect it was Petrov both times, using the same warehouse as some kind of personal homage for his revenge."

"Do you believe it was Petrov who took out our team then? It sounds like he'd be capable." Felix says.

"No…I don't, I believe there was a high probability it actually was the Tsiatko." Reggie replies. "But I believe Allmass was actually stalling, waiting in San Francisco for Petrov. Maybe waiting until he had this last job done. I'm not sure but…I think Allmass is not alone. Whatever he's doing, Petrov, Smirnov whatever you want to call him, is with Allmass."

"But why would Allmass let him go then send a hit team after him?'

"Testing him maybe?" Reggie says.

"Then why would this Petrov, Smirnov, agree to work for Allmass?"

"Probably for the money. He's a gun for hire. Maybe Allmass offered him a ton of cash."

"So, what do you take from all this?" Felix asks.

"I would say that if Allmass is after the Orb, he has this assassin helping him and he may even have others. You better warn your teams because if they go after Allmass without this information, things are going to get messy."

CHAPTER EIGHT

It's just after one in the morning as Frank takes the I-90 directly into Seattle and with Zach navigating they head to an industrial area. Oin, still lying on the bench watching, looks over at Gaylord. He and his co-Handlers decided to re-intervene when it became blatantly aware it was the powerful, the corrupt and the greedy that were planning to abandon this planet to save their own necks, unlike the previous relocations orchestrated by the Handlers to actually preserve mankind but now, Oin is having second thoughts over his decision to participate so active-ly. As a Handler, he's only suppose to influence from the shadows. He lives for a two hundred year cycle, the average lifespan humans will eventually attain then regenerates through cloning to continue on. For him, the memories of that have been lost in time. It's been play, repeat, play then repeat. He has no recollection how many thousands of times he's gone through that process. He's tired of it, so much so he's taking this risk by coming along hoping it will change things and possibly give him something to remember. He's concerned now that what if this choice of his somehow has a negative irreversible impact on Frank's mission, something that can't be undone? Christ, Willow is going to rip him a good one when she catches up with him.

Frank makes a hard turn, disrupting Oin's thoughts and jostling everyone in the van. They're now on Sixth Avenue South, cruising, watching for United Warehouses just off of Holgate. As Zach has explained it, the Committee has warehouse space there for storing arms and other special needs equipment; what exactly special needs entails, Frank's not sure.

They spot it and do a few drive bys before choosing to try a single lane entrance way past the warehouse just after an education building that's butted against it. They find themselves in the parking lot of a Credit Union directly behind the warehouse, invisible from the street. They stop, facing the warehouse. With the warehouse and education center forming a large L to their right and chain link fencing next to a rail line on the left, they're in the centre of a U shaped barrier which provides complete privacy for their task. The down side is that they only have one way out.

"The warehouse looks pitch black inside, no lights anywhere and I didn't see any security." Frank says a bit bewildered.

Oin pokes his head up front. "Seriously Z, are you sure this is it, doesn't look like any place to stash guns, maybe we should call it off?"

"Oin, you're just here for the ride, remember that." Frank says curtly and gets back to the task at hand.

"Yea, the smug assholes." Zach says. "Hide things in plain sight as the saying goes. They have a couple cameras out front and a private security firm that patrols the area occasionally. Back here, nothing. Why would they? It's solid concrete walls." And winks.

They peer through the windshield at the warehouse.

"See that window about fifteen feet up? That's the hallway between two of the back storage areas. We can enter there then it's a short distance to the main corridor, we turn right and about a hundred feet is the unit we want." Zach states.

"Dude, how we gonna break through those walls man? We got nothing." Oin asks, still playing the role.

Frank smiles. "Oin, we've got everything we need right in here. We got Gaylord."

Gaylord still looks a bit out of it and simply gives another thumb up sign.

"Are you alright?" Frank asks him.

"Yes, my friend, I am fine. You need not worry. Your ritual had an effect on me bit I will do what is needed of me." Gaylord says.

Zach jumps out and opens the rear doors and Frank backs up the van snug against the warehouse wall where Zach indicated. Zach climbs back in through the side door. "Are you ready for this Frank? At least you know what's coming, for me; this scares the crap out of me." He says half jokingly.

"Zach, you're about to have the experience of your life." Frank laughs.

"How are we going to do this?" Zach asks.

"Oin, you get the job of staying with the van. You'll have no way to reach us so if something comes up out here just drive away, wait a half hour than come back and park in this same spot, the same way. Got it?" Frank says.

"Sure, but I still don't get what's going on man, I mean … like how you getting in?" Oin asks.

"Just sit back and watch … and don't get too worked up about whatever you see." Frank says. "Zach, we'll let Gaylord get in first as he'll have to crawl his way though from the van. Then we can take turns as he pulls us through. Oin, if all goes good, you be ready to assist with anything we feed back, okay?"

"What do you mean feed through … through what Frank?" Oin asks.

"Like I said, just watch and wait … and no smoking, got it?"

"Yea, yea, I got it." Oin replies.

Gaylord lines up head first and pushes himself through the wall. A fraction of a second later he pokes his head into view. "Trouble!" He announces as he simultaneously grabs Frank and Zach and yanks them through. Then, all hell breaks loose.

CHAPTER NINE

Frank and Zach land hard on the warehouse floor. The corridors in the warehouse are lit up like Christmas trees. The windows have been blacked out. They're at the end of a tee intersection just fifty from the primary one. As they stand, an armed man walks by and spots them. He yells out. There's no time to think, only react. Gaylord reaches him in two monstrous strides, crushing him against a wall, breaking through it and landing twenty feet into the next room. Frank and Zach follow. They hear shouting coming from farther down the main passageway.

"Find them!" Frank yells to Gaylord pointing to the general direction of the sounds. "I'll take care of anyone coming down the hallway!" As he grabs the automatic from the guards belt along with extra clips.

Gaylord takes the "shortcut" through any of the impeding walls and barriers to do as he was instructed, searching for his assigned targets.

Frank checks that he has a round in the chamber as he scrambles back to the hallway. "Stay behind me!" he yells to Zach. Frank hits the corridor running, firing a continual volley of rounds. He fires, reloads, fires, never slowing down, never missing a beat, dropping each assailant with head shots until they arrive at the entrance to the intended storage room. He suspects some of his targets were attacking, others just trying to escape Gaylord's wrath. Frank stops, signaling Zach to do the same as he quickly peeks inside before entering.

Zach follows to see Gaylord, chest arched out, his arms spread letting out a loud triumphant roar that rattles the windows in the room. There're bloody patterns against the walls and racking where Gaylord must have tossed his opponents, only to have their bodies crushed against the unyielding materials. Others on the ground look that they've been stomped by the massive Tsiatko or pummeled by his wrecking ball-like fists. There's carnage everywhere. Zach pushes passed Frank to inspect the downed group. "Shit Frank, these are the guys I led." He does a quick count of the bodies in the room and out in the hallway. He comes rushing back in. "Frank, there's two teams here. They must've gearing up for a mission… probably at Rainier, for me. There's no other reason they'd be here. These guys are good but you got the drop on them. They weren't prepared for an attack like this. Christ… no one would be prepared for an assault like this."

Frank walks farther in. It looks like most in here were gathered around a large table which is now busted up, lying on its side when Gaylord made his entrance. He sifts through the blood spattered debris of papers, maps and pictures and finds copies of his Sherriff's I.D. and his Petrov passport. "What the fuck is this?!" He wonders picking them up.

"Frank, we got to load up now! If these guys were here without transport… that can only mean there are more teams on their way! Grab that cart over there!" Zach yells out.

Frank shoves the pictures in his jacket and does as he's told. Zach grabs some duffle bags off the pallet raking and starts throwing in a variety of weapons and gear, zipping each one closed as he's finished, leaving Frank to load them on the cart. "Frank grab those large ammo boxes, throw them on another cart and follow me. Gaylord take that load to Oin, now!" Zach orders and Gaylord doesn't hesitate. Frank follows as Zach fills the boxes with assorted ammunition until they're nearly full. "Ok, we don't have any more time, take these and I'll be right behind you!"

Frank runs down the hallway pushing the cart, weaving his way around the bodies ignoring their weapons scattered in the hallway. He hears Zach behind him and turns to see him running hard carrying two rifle cases. They get to the wall where Gaylord is waiting and he feeds through the boxes and then the two cases of Zach's. He passes Frank and Zach through first, then himself.

"What the hell is all this and what happened in there?!" Oin yells back from the driver's seat.

"Oin," Frank shouts. "Just shut the fuck up and drive ok?! Now's not the time!" As he and Zach take a seat on the bench.

Oin guns the powerful engine and they're careening with each sharp turn. Frank and Zach say nothing; their minds are too engrossed in replaying what just happened behind the warehouse wall that's just disappeared from their view.

Gaylord is smiling at Frank. It's because of his eyes. Frank can feel they've turned. Gaylord pats Frank's knee. "It is good to see you back with us Brother." Obviously his eye change has significance to the Tsiatko.

Its three a.m. and the streets are empty of traffic. Oin is giving it all it's worth. They hit the I-90 and Oin floors it. Frank opens one of the bags and sees Zach has loaded plenty of fire power. He finds a handgun with a full clip and shoves it in his belt. As this stage he doesn't care who gets in their way, the Committee, the cops, he's prepared to take out whoever he needs to. Fortunately, nothing does and forty-five minutes later Oin busts through the chain hung across the parking lot entrance where their adventure began. Oin screeches to a stop near where they were first parked. He isn't worried about concealment. He jumps out and opens the back door. Frank gets out first and grabs Oin.

"Forget the van just get the hell out of here, now!" Frank demands and as those words leave his mouth, a black Lexus SUV tears into the lot. Frank draws his weapon and is about to fire at the on-coming vehicle when Oin jumps in front.

"No!" Oin screams.

It approaches and skids to a stop ten feet away, Stogie Man is behind the wheel. A woman jumps out from the passenger side and opens the back passenger door. "Oin, get in!" She yells.

"Willow!" Oin calls as he turns.

Frank has to look twice. This isn't the Silent Willow he knows. This one is a knockout. Oin climbs in the back of the Lexus and Willow gets back in without saying another word, calmly watching Frank as the SUV reverses hard into a bootleg and then takes off. Frank turns back to the van. Gaylord already has an ammo box in each hand and two duffle bags slung over his shoulders.

"Don't wait for us, just go." Franks instructs him.

Zach already has the two rifle cases and waits as Frank grabs the last duffle bag. "Who was that?"Zach asks.

Frank looks back one final time. "You wouldn't believe me if I told you." He replies before heading towards the cave, Zach is right beside him.

As they move past the trees, they can't see Gaylord but they're sure he's probably already there. They run with their loads and ten minutes later they arrive at the entrance, Gaylord is waiting for them as well as Brother who utters a few grunts and whistles and a team of Tsiatko, including Gaylord start clearing the entrance way.

"What're you doing?" Zach asks. "That's the only thing blocking the way."

"I know." Brother says.

"Frank?" Zach says, confusion showing on his face.

"We will do this my way." Brother commands. "I want them to come. Your job is to draw them in. Once they are inside, we will take care of matters."

The Tsiatko are ripping apart the trees and massive roots as if they're twigs and discard them off to each side of the exterior, the same for the boulders, creating a funnel. With the pathway clear and with Gaylord's help, they haul all the cargo inside. Frank and Zach recover their headlamps from the corner and sort through it all, selecting a variety of items, putting them into one duffle bag. Zach reaches back in a bag and grabs the concealable Kevlar vests, handing two of them to Frank.

"That should do it Gaylord." Frank says. "The rest take and put by our tents."

Hang on," Zach adds, "We'll need these." As he grabs the two gun cases. "Oh, just a sec," And tosses Gaylord their PVC suits followed by their backpacks. The Tsiatko depart including Brother and Gaylord.

Frank and Zach take the time to don two vests each, better to be on the safe side.

"I guess they aren't that concerned about me anymore, not that I'd have anywhere to go. What now?" Zach asks.

"We do what the man says; we get ready and draw them in." Frank replies.

CHAPTER TEN

Felix is woken by knocking on his bedroom door. "Come in!" he calls out as he looks over at his bedside clock, it's four a.m.

Bertram enters. "Sir, we have a situation with the teams."

"What kind?"

"Serious."

"How serious?"

"It's serious enough to wake you at," Bertram replies, checking his watch, "Four o three in the morning sir."

"Fine." Felix says as he struggles to get out. Bertram rushes over to assist. "I'll need twenty minutes then meet me in my office….oh, which is the most senior of the Team Leaders?"

"I'm not sure sir, I haven't orientated myself on that information yet."

"Well, find out and have him on line when I get to my office. Tell him I expect an update on matters when I get there."

"Yes sir." Bertram answers and leaves.

Felix shuffles his way to the washroom. "I am getting too old for this shit." As Felix exits his bedroom, Garth Scott, his Chief of Security, is waiting outside his door.

Scott is attired as he always is, in a two piece grey linen suit of one shade or another and a black dress shirt. Scott is…different. He stands at six feet four inches, lean with a dark black Amish style beard. He has Cossack style hair which is a long lock growing from the top of his otherwise bald head. This braided lock, as Scott has explained in the past, must hang on the left side of his head, a requirement of his ancestral superstitions. Scott believes an angel always sits on his right shoulder and the devil on his left, the forelock tail's task is to constantly brush the devil off so that Scott will always be on the side of the righteous. He has odd looks and strange beliefs but he's done a hell of a job Felix believes. He was highly recommended by Reggie when his previous security head passed a year ago from heart failure.

"Scott. We haven't talked in awhile." Felix says. Felix rarely refers to his people by their first names, Reggie is an exception.

"I'm doing well Mr. Belette. I apologize for intruding but considering what's been going on, I feel more comfortable sticking a little closer to you until we have some answers." Scott says speaking with an Aussie accent which doesn't match his Cossack look. Even after twelve months of interaction with him, his manner of speech still takes Felix off guard.

"Your call, that's what I pay you for." Felix says.

His key personnel understand that they're paid well to do their job and not to bother him unless the situation is dire. They're all aware of the consequences if they fail. Scott escorts Felix as they stroll to the other wing where his office is located.

"What is going on, as you put it?" Felix asks.

"I'd rather not speculate sir and cause any undue stress as I really have not been privy to any specifics yet." Scott answers.

Felix nods and walks on. He'll know soon enough. He enters his office to see Bertram and Reggie already seated in front of his desk. Scott elects to remain standing just inside the door. "Reggie, how are you this early morning?" Felix asks.

"Fine, thank you."

Felix continues in and takes a seat at his desk. "Bertram, which Team Leader is on the line?"

"Curtis Ramsey, sir."

Felix puts him on speaker phone. "Ramsey?"

Yes, Mr. Belette." Ramsey replies.

"Here's the deal. Since we have a "situation" now and Allmass is no longer your boss, I will be giving my directives in regards to the field operations through you since you have the most seniority. Do you have an issue with that?" Felix asks.

"No sir."

"Good answer." Felix responds. "What've we got?"

'We lost two teams sir." Ramsey states.

"How?"

"We don't know sir, violently is all I can add."

Felix is taken aback by the comment. "What do you mean you don't know how?"

"Of the five teams you ordered to find Allmass, two of them were gearing up from our supply depot in Seattle. When the other teams arrived to transport them, they found everyone dead."

Bertram hands Felix a folder. "These are the photos of the scene sent to us from Seattle."

Felix peruses through them. They show the damaged hallway and adjacent room, the bodies scattered in the corridor and show the carnage and slaughter house in their supply area. Felix looks up in disbelief. Who the hell did this?!"

"We don't know sir." Ramsey says. "The casualties in the hallway were shot. We have no idea what happened to the rest of them."

Felix leans back in his chair. "Are you telling me, someone penetrated one our supposedly secure sites, wiped out two specially trained teams and ... we don't know a goddamn thing!" He says tossing the pictures on his desk.

"Mr. Belette." Reggie speaks up. "Considering our last meeting, the individuals we were discussing and the proximity of this incident to Rainier, I took the liberty of investigating some other avenues while everyone else was doing what they needed to do." She hands Felix a file. "You have very dedicated men working for you in the field. I only accumulated this a few minutes before you arrived but took the liberty of emailing them to Mr. Ramsey as I felt it would be prudent for him to have them for this meeting."

Felix opens the dossier to find additional photographs. "What's this?" He asks as he flips through them.

"These are security pictures taken from an ATM located behind the ware-house facility where the depot is located. The vehicle is unique, appears to be a early nineteen fifties delivery van that's been customized. As the time lapse pictures show, it appears to be Allmass exiting the vehicle, opening the rear doors, which then backs against the warehouse wall. It looks like Smirnov is driving." Reggie reaches across and sifts through the pictures to ones time stamped a half hour later. "Approximately thirty minutes later, the vehicle speeds away with an unknown male now driving."

"Do you have these Ramsey?' Felix asks.

"Yes sir."

"Were these two men found in the warehouse?"

"No sir."

Felix looks up at the pair seated in front of him. "So why did they park there, wait and then leave and where are they now?" He asks to no one in particular.

"Sir," Ramsey speaks out. "The remaining three teams searched the entire complex and no one else was found. We checked the security tapes for the front cameras and no one exited there."

"Is there anything missing?" Felix asks him.

"Well it's still too early a hundred percent accurate but based on a preliminary inventory," They can hear Curtis flipping through papers, "Approximately half a dozen Glock 9mms, two Atchisson Assault Shotguns, two XM2010 sniper rifles, four M4 collapsible carbines…uh, two additional shotguns with bean bag rounds, four Kevlar vests, binoculars, a couple sets of night vision goggles and a few thousand rounds of assorted ammunition are unaccounted for…oh, and two Mag-Guns. There could be more, we're not sure." He says.

"Oh, so relatively nothing!" Felix shouts and pounds on the desk. "What the fuck kind of bullshit is this?!" He yells. "Where are these weapons?!"

"We don't know sir." Ramsey replies. "We do know all the inventory was accounted for before the teams arrived."

"So let me recap everything." Felix barks out. "We have two trained experienced teams down, what…twenty men in total? We have a large supply of weapons and ammo gone, who knows where. On the other end, we have three individuals, two of them our prime targets, backing up to a concrete wall right next to our facility for no known reason…speeding off after our teams are assassinated and a massive amount of weapons are gone in a hot rod…Reggie, am I missing anything?"

"No Mr. Belette." Reggie says.

"I hope the fuck not!" He shouts glaring at the pair seated in front of him, reluctantly taking the brunt of his anger. "Do we actually know anything, make sense of anything?!"

"No disrespect sir," Ramsey speaks up before anyone else can respond, "But to be candid the reason we don't know a goddamn thing is because we…I have never come across circumstances as strange this in my entire career and I'm not sure if I ever will."

There's an awkward silence. It's broken by an aide bursting into the room. Any further advance of his is blocked by Scott who releases him once he recognizes him. "For your own safety, knock next time, got it?" Scott says.

The aide looks a bit flushed and nods his acknowledgement. "Sir, you need to see this." As the aide rushes to hand several photographs to Felix.

"What are these?" Felix asks.

"These are photos from various traffic cameras along the I-90 as well as satellite images taken around four a.m. at Mt. Rainier National Park. Thermal satellite imagery from Rainier shows a vehicle similar in shape to the delivery van in Seattle pulling into the parking lot. Then two individuals get out as another vehicle, probably an SUV pulls in. One person steps out of the SUV and one of the trio from the van enters the SUV. The person that stepped out re-enters the SUV and it leaves." He explains.

Felix starts passing them around.

"Then," The aide continues, "Two individuals from the van appear to extract something from inside and proceed on foot about a mile and then disappear, probably into a cave or bluff. It's been confirmed that the van is still on location at Rainier."

"Ramsey." Felix says. "Did you hear all that?"

"Yes sir."

"Bertram, provide our messenger here," Felix says indicating the aide, "Ramsey's contact info. Scan and send these to him ASAP."

"Yes sir." The aide says and departs once Bertram hands him the information.

Felix looks to Reggie for a silent confirmation.

"Almass and Smirnov." She says nodding.

"Who had the forethought to do this?" Felix asks.

Bertram looks to Ms. Byrnes.

"I did Mr. Belette." Reggie says. "When I saw the direction the suspect vehicle was heading, we hacked into the traffic cameras to further verify their intended destination may be Rainier, I then believed there was a high probability that something could be tracked by Satellite at Rainier, especially this time of day."

"Of course you would." Felix replies.

"I'd say it's the unidentified male driver who gets into the SUV so that would make at least three other individuals assisting Allmass and Smirnov. Who they are we haven't a clue. I'm having the driver's image from the ATM cleaned up and run through all the facial recognition data bases we have available." Reggie says.

"Good thinking." Felix replies. "Ramsey, how soon can we get our people to Rainier?"

"They're good to go sir." Curtis says.

Felix drops his head slightly as he thinks, running his fingers through his thinning white hair and yawns.

"Are you alright?" Reggie asks.

"Yes, just tired." He replies as he gets up and walks to window for a moment. Felix notices the movement of light on the grounds. Scott must have added extra guards. He bobs his head ever so slightly before turning back to face them. "Bertram, contact our people in Homeland Security and have them reach out to the Ashford Sherriff's Office and inform them that there are NSA Tactical Units enroute to Mt. Rainier National Park. Advise them that they're tracking a known terrorist that's holed up in the park and that this individual is also a suspect in the disappearance of their Deputy Frank Smirnov." Felix takes his seat again. "Also have them instruct the Sherriff's office that they're to secure the entire park boundary but not to proceed into the park due to the ensuing manhunt. Also tell them that if the public or media asks why, they're to tell them that recent seismic activity is suggesting there's a real possibility of an eruption at Mt. Rainier." Felix looks to Reggie. "Reggie, contact our people in the FAA and have an advisory issued restricting all air traffic within an eighty mile radius of Mt. Rainier using the potential eruption as the reason. That should give enough privacy to do what needs to be done." Felix says. "We'll deal with any blowback later." He takes one last browse through all the information on his desk. "Ok then." Felix says. "That should cover it. Ramsey, contact the teams in Seattle and tell them they have a green light but emphasize that I still want every effort to have Allmass brought in alive. They can break him a bit, but alive. It's open season on anyone else that may be in his company. Anyone have anything else?"

"I do." Ramsey says.

"What is it?" Felix asks impatiently.

"The Tsiatko are a credible threat, we've hunted them enough to know. We have to consider the teams may encounter them at Rainier. Look what happened at Trinity Alps where a single Tsiatko may have taken out the entire unit. What happens with this assault if they encounter a larger force of them? I strongly believe this is a real and potential possibility. Look at some of these pictures from Seattle. In my opinion, Allmass or any human associate of his, is not capable of inflicting this type of damage."

"Are you trying to suggest one of these creatures participated in taking out the teams in Seattle, how?" Felix asks.

"I don't have an answer for that but look at the pictures." Ramsey says.

Felix relents. "What're you suggesting then?" He asks.

"I want the teams to stand down once they reach Rainier until the rest of our squads arrive along with the new drone unit. We'll need about two hours. We send in the drones first, capture any images of what we're up against and then it's a full blown assault with maximum numbers for maximum results and minimum casualties." Ramsey says. He knows the drone unit is mandatory for all their field operations now ever since Trinity. He hates the high tech involvement but orders are orders. Although this directive came through Felix, it was the Committee itself who specifically stipulated this.

Felix ponders this recommendation for a few moments. "I'll agree but, to let you know, that by designating all of our teams to this one effort you're guaranteeing me results." Felix adds.

"I understand." Curtis replies.

"I'm sure you're aware of my reputation. If you're not successful, you WILL become a disposable asset. Am I clear on this?" Felix says.

"You are sir." Curtis confirms.

"Then get at it." Felix says. "I want an end to this today.

CHAPTER ELEVEN

Stogie Man keeps glancing in the rear view mirror at Oin as the three of them speed away from Rainier. Oin is avoiding his scowls by looking out the side window. Stogie Man looks over at Willow, he can't believe she's holding back. It doesn't last much longer. Willow turns to face Oin, who's fidgeting in the back seat.

"Look, I know I screwed up, I'm sorry." Oin blurts out.

"Screwed up? You went beyond screwed up. I…I don't even know where to begin?" Willow replies.

"I know but." Oin says.

"But nothing, shut up!" She orders, cutting him off.

"I've been getting that a lot lately." He mutters under his breath.

"What?!" Willow demands.

"Nothing, I didn't say a damn thing." Oin answers.

"Exactly." She responds. "Do you have any idea about all the possible scenarios that have been going through our heads? We didn't know if you were dead, in the hands of the Committee….or what, you were just gone. What were you thinking taking off with them?"

Oin leans forward to answer but before he can say a thing, Willow scolds him some more.

"We're more than Handlers; we're a team, family. You two are like brothers to me. We have been together for so long, it's like you are a physical part of me. Can you understand that? Do you have any idea of that concept? And don't, don't say anything about it being because I'm a woman otherwise I'm going to rip your heart out like you just did to mine with your actions!"

Oin sits back silently, looking down. Stogie Man says nothing as he knows better after all these eons.

"I know," Oin finally says looking up. "But I couldn't help myself. I like Frank and I just wanted to be participating with someone other than ourselves. Actually do something rather than steering someone all the time. I was tired of the old way but man… I soon realized I was over my head."

What do mean?" Stogie Man asks.

"I really don't know what went on as I was in the van the entire time but we hit this place in Seattle… with a Tsiatko and." Oin says.

Stogie Man looks back quick. "You met a Tsiatko?" he interjects.

"Yea," Oin chuckles, "It was unbelievable."

Willow glances at Stogie Man before returning her attention to Oin. "Seattle?" She reminds him, to get him back on track even though part of her wants to know more about the Tsiatko.

"Look, all I know is that the three of them were passing back and forth through solid concrete walls and we ending up loading a serious pile of weapons before bee-lining it back here." Oin says.

"No shit." Stogie Man remarks.

"Three of them, who are the three of them?" Willow asks.

"Frank, the Tsiatko and that guy Zachariah, you know Allmass?"

"Huh." Willow says as she turns facing the front.

"What?" Stogie Man asks her.

"What?" Oin repeats as he leans forward.

"We all know," She begins as she turns toward them, "That without the Orb, we've been flying blind to a certain degree. Without it, we have no clear direction and no parameters to use as benchmarks. We've been trying to go by memory but there have been so many annexations; they all seem to blend together. Too many and too much time from start to finish. All we do know is that Frank eventually gets possession of the Orb and we need to be there when he does."

"That's why we've been monitoring him and helping as best we can." Oin says.

"And when he has it," Stogie Man adds, "We take it back."

"I know that WAS the plan but… things may change. Why is Zachariah in on things now? He led the charge against the Tsiatko on behalf of the Committee.

Why…how is it the Tsiatko are okay with him being involved? It doesn't add up." Willow says.

"I haven't a clue. Hey…I did get stoned with a Tsiatko though." Oin says grinning. "Even got to name him, Gaylord."

"What?!" Willow asks glancing back but before he can reply, she turns away. "I don't want to know right now." She massages her forehand before turning back to Oin. "Frank looked alright, he's okay isn't he? He didn't get hurt or anything?"

"Yea…he's fine. Why?" Oin asks

"Just making sure." As she turns back to the front. She can feel her face blush. She understands Oin's comment about Frank. She likes him as well. He made quite an impression on her even though she was seating in the back seat, not really saying a word, the first time they officially met. Or maybe it's because it's been so long since she had any interaction with a man other than these two. But she has been watching him from afar for quite some time, before their meet and ever since. "I wonder how he would feel about a dominant "older" woman." She asks herself and unknowingly laughs out loud. She catches herself and glances at Stogie Man, "What?"

"Nothing…I'm just driving." Stogie Man says as he peers at Oin in the rear view mirror. Oin shakes his head and shrugs his shoulders in response.

"Good, keep driving." Willow orders.

CHAPTER TWELVE

Curtis Ramsey is riding shotgun in the lead vehicle as they approach the parking lot entrance at Mt. Rainier. His convoy of seventeen Humvees comes to a brief halt as they wait for the Deputy Sheriffs to move their vehicles barricading it.

A Deputy bundled up in a sheepskin coat, gloves and felt hat waves them through. "Go get him guys! Get him for Frank, hear me, for Frank!" He yells as they move past.

Ramsey gives a smile and a thumb up sign but shakes his head at their gullibility at believing the terrorist cover story. The fact is, their "fallen comrade" Frank is still alive and holed up here with Allmass but will soon be collateral damage. They park near the dozen Humvees that arrived earlier transporting the other teams and sees they've completed setting up the large insulated tent to use as a Command Centre. Ramsey steps out of his Humvee. He's not a big man, average size, average weight and average looks, but looks can be deceiving. He's known for his voracity at getting the job done and the men respect him. His men know what is required of them and they begin checking their weapons and unloading gear in preparation of what's coming. Ramsey, followed by the four Team Leaders traveling with him, head to the tent.

"What the fuck bullshit is this making us stand down til you got here, Ramsey?" One of the Team Leaders from Seattle demands as they enter.

Curtis gives him a cold stare. "Shut the fuck up…and if you speak to me like that again," As he draws a large bladed knife from his belt, "I'll slit your throat and watch you bleed out like a stuck pig. Am I clear?" He says.

"Christ…cool down…you weren't there, you didn't see what those mothers did." Is the reply.

"You'll get your payback. Now gather round." Ramsey barks out.

Ramsey, the seven Team Leaders and Richard Montgomery, the head of the drone unit assemble around a table with a topographical map of the area.

"First off, if anyone has an issue that our primary target being Allmass, speak up now. This is no time for old allegiances." Ramsey orders.

There are only shakes of the head, no one says a thing.

"This isn't a typical hunt but Montgomery's team is still in on this one." Ramsey says.

There are only silent acknowledgements from all. All those here and present including the team members outside that comprise this force have no respect for these military nerds. To them, Montgomery and his pilots have not proven their worth, if fact, most believe they're of little value. They're a compulsory inclusion for all their tactical maneuvers now and the teams believe their involvement is more about monitoring them than anything else. Montgomery is well aware of everyone's opinions as many have been quite vocal about it.

"Okay, I don't have to remind everyone about Trinity Alps. There's a high risk of encountering the Tsiatko here so we aren't taking chances. Montgomery's team will do the recon in the cave our targets are suspected of being holed up." Ramsey says. "This operation may get complicated. These cave systems may go on for miles into the mountain. There's the possibility there are a number of entrances and exit points. We can't do any recon by helicopter because of the no fly zone restriction it would only raise red flags since we've warned of a pending eruption. We're counting on Montgomery's team to penetrate the cave as far as they can and get us a green light."

Montgomery's team consists of him and three UAV pilots. One of their Humvee carries the gear; the other is set up with three operating stations, one for each pilot and for ease of communication between them by all being contained in a single Humvee. Their drones are the latest technology, small and strictly for reconnaissance equipped with thermal sensors, night vision and live video feed which is recorded as well.

A Team Leader from Seattle speaks up. "We did verify a set of Tsiatko tracks as well as two sets of boot prints leading to and from this parking lot in the direction of the cave entrance tagged by the Satellite images. Not that we had any recent shots to work with but comparing old to new, the entrance appears to have been cleared of any debris that may have been blocking it and it's now stacked outside the entrance…looks fresh."

"Were there signs of more than one Tsiatko?" Ramsey asks.

"We weren't able to track much more than a few hundred feet toward the cave, there's only one set and it's a big mother. We can't be sure how many are already inside." The Leader replies.

"Our advantage," Ramsey says, "Is that we have no open ground to deal with. This is strictly close quarters combat which gives us an edge, no surprise attacks this way. A search and destroy mission. Allmass and the other target is armed but I don't believe they're prepared for the numbers we're going to throw at them. The down side is that the boss has made it very clear Allmass has to be taken alive. Battered if need be but alive."

"So, the standard side arms, shotguns and M4s?" A Team Leader asks for confirmation as the weapons of choice for this mission.

"Correct." Ramsey says. "Montgomery, are the Mag-Guns a concern?"

"Of course but it really depends if they get sight of the drones. These ones we use are pretty compact, a hard target. We'll have to wait and see." Montgomery says.

"That's a shit answer Montgomery. Our necks are on the line geek." A Team Leader says.

"Hey," Montgomery begins before being cut off by Ramsey.

"Can it, like the man said, we'll have to wait and see." Ramsey orders.

"Bullshit!" The Belligerent Team Leader replies as he approaches Ramsey, "Fucking bullshit! Bullshit that they sit back in their comfy Humvee spying on us with their high end toys! We all know they're not really here to help and what's wrong with using our good old tried and true ways!"

"And how good did that work at Trinity?!" Ramsey yells back coming face to face with Belligerent.

"You know…we all know, the end result at Trinity had nothing to do with how we did our hunts!" Belligerent shouts back.

Ramsey takes a step back and looks at the men circling the table. They're all giving him that knowing look; that Belligerent is finally voicing what they all know.

Belligerent comes in close to Ramsey. "I even heard it from Allmass himself. He thought he was alone out there in Trinity. He was spouting off to them after we lost the team…yelling at them out in the mountains, ranting, saying he knew…he knew they were just testing us but couldn't figure out why, until now." Belligerent says in a hard, hoarse tone.

"And why wold he be going off like that?" Ramsey asks dryly.

"I don't know…I got called back before he finished!" Belligerent answers, turning to face those at the table. "But we all know its bullshit we put any of those things down! You saw…we all saw how fast they can move! There's no way we should have caught up with them but we did. We didn't care how or fucking why…we were fighting again, having fun doing it and getting wads of cash thrown at us!"

"So…what…the fuck…is your point?!" Ramsey demands.

Belligerent leans on the table and takes a big breath; he can't hide it, he's scared. "Fucking Seattle…you didn't see it, you didn't smell it. It's in my goddamn clothes." He says violently yanking on his jacket. "Its footprints were in their blood, I wanted proof to remind myself that these things…I don't know what but I didn't take any pics; that's the rule." He looks back up at Ramsey. "That fucker was huge and he tore our guys apart like nothing…they didn't even have a chance to fire back, that same son of a bitch is here, what if all of them here are like that?"

Ramsey eyes the rest of the Team Leaders. He can see the fear in their eyes but they aren't afraid, they're not standing down…only Belligerent is showing weakness. He grabs Belligerent by the back of his collar and hoists him upright. "You want to be a pussy, be a pussy. Leave…run with your tail between your legs but guess what?" Ramsay says as he pulls Belligerent in close and tight, "You'll never look in the mirror again." He whispers before shoving him away. "Man up bitch! They're blood and bone boy, blood and bone!" He shouts. "Now take off those panties and get back around this table."

Belligerent takes a moment to breathe and compose himself. "Sorry boss." He says nodding and takes his place.

To Montgomery, this is the craziest exchange he's ever witnessed. These guys are fucking nuts.

"The =perimeter?" Another Team Leader asks as if nothing went on.

"We're leaving that for the Sherriff's Department. They're out in full force and have the place closed off including patrols with orders not to permit anyone in or out, regardless." Ramsey answers.

"What about sniper fire?" Another Leader asks.

Ramsey points to the location of the cave entrance on the map. "The terrain overall is fairly flat and accessible so we'll head out wide, give no clear target and come in from the sides. The lead team will launch in a few concussion grenades and then we enter." He says.

"And how do we take down Allmass battered but alive?" Another Leader says.

"Two of the lead team will have bean bag rounds in their shotguns." Curtis answers. Bean bag rounds are a small fabric pillow filled with lead shot that distributes upon impact, does not penetrate the body or cause long term trauma and leaves the target immobile.

"Yea … the guys are going to love that news." The Leader replies.

"Tell them to suck it up." Ramsey states.

"So we're not holding anyone back?" Another Leader asks.

"Affirmative," Ramsey says. "We're all in. Any issues with that?"

Again there's silence.

"Okay, enough with the chit chat," Ramsey says sarcastically, "Rock n roll." As he exits the Command tent, every team member is geared up and waiting, showing their support as there was no way they could avoid hearing the exchange from within. He gives them an appraising look. "Semper Fi!" He shouts.

"Oorah!" Is the deafening reply.

CHAPTER THIRTEEN

From the safety of the dark in the cave, Frank gazes at the scene below through binoculars. Zach is beside him doing the same. They'd seen the first set of Humvees roll in and now another convoy of them has arrived.

"Christ Zach," Frank says as he lowers the binoculars, "How many of them did they send?"

Zach continues to watch the activity. "I think every team. That'd be eighty of them. And it looks like they have a drone unit with them as well which is not unexpected. They added them to all the hunts after Trinity." He says.

"How'd you know that?" Frank asks.

Zach drops the binoculars. "Not everyone down there quit talking to me after I left." He says smiling. "I didn't think they'd be throwing everyone at us though." He's surprised as that's not Felix's style.

"Is that going to be a problem?"

"Don't ask me. Ask your buddy in there. He's the one who said to draw them in."

Frank takes a couple steps forward to get a better view and scans the area with his binoculars again. "I don't see any media out there, no helicopters in the air… why?" Before dropping them back down.

"I'm sure they came up with some kind of creative cover story." Zach remarks.

"Well…these were your teams, how're they going to come at us?"

"I'm not sure who's calling the shots now on the ground, probably Ramsey. He's been around the longest and he's good." Zach says.

"And who above him is directing things then since you're out of the picture?" Frank asks.

"That would be good old Felix Belette. The appointed spokesperson for the Committee. The guy is ruthless and smart. He earned the nickname Weasel back in the day and liked it so much he changed his name to incorporate it." Zach says as he turns to Frank. "Belette is French for weasel."

"What was it before?"

"Reeseman."

"Reeseman? Why does that name ring a bell?"

"General Reeseman headed up the Roswell project. You might remember him from Mr. H's journals. Belette was his son."

"Son? How old is this guy?"

"Old. He's the one suspected of blowing up the Solomons' lab in order to stop them from creating you. If he only knew."

"He may know more than you think." Frank says.

"What do you mean?"

Frank takes out the pictures he recovered from the warehouse in Seattle and hands them to Zach.

"Where'd you get these?"

"At the warehouse where we took out the teams. They were in the area where Gaylord did his handy work."

"How's this possible?" Zach asks, staring down at the photographs.

"I don't know but we have to assume Belette knows more than you think. The teams down there as well."

"Impossible, I didn't leave a trail anywhere."

"You should know by now, nothing's impossible." Frank says as he takes the pictures back and tucks them away. "So…what do we do?"

Zach sits down on his haunches, resting his arms on his thighs. "Here's how I see it. It's not my style but they'll send in the drones first, they're strictly recon and not armed, to try and get a layout of what they're up against. As the drones are dispatched, the teams will be deployed in a wide circle away from any direct line of fire that we could disperse from here." Zach says. He then stands and looks at the entrance from different angles from the inside. "Based on what the Tsiatko have done, once the teams are in place outside, they'll probably toss in a few concussion grenades to disorient us and then hit us head on. Sending in everyone they've got. That's how I read it." Zach turns back to Frank. "How many Tsiatko do you think Brother has here?"

"I haven't a clue. I saw…maybe thirty but there could be more. He seems pretty confident."

"Hopefully not over confident." Zach says. "That's a lot of firepower they're going against."

Zach takes out a sniper rifle out of the bag. "Here, you're the hot shot marksman." And tosses it to Frank followed by a bundle of full clips.

"And do what?"

"Let our presence be known."

"And what're you going to be doing?"

Zach smiles as he opens one of the rifle cases. He pulls out a weapon that looks like a combination machine gun and…who knows what. It's large with a variety of electronics and coils visible from a plexi glass like panel on its side.

"What the fuck is that?" Frank asks.

"This, my friend, is an Automatic Electromagnetic Pulse Rifle. It's a spin off from one the private sector partner's Champ Program…based on more of the good old Roswell technology recovered. This bad boy generates an EMP pulse that can fire fifteen shots per two seconds and will fry out the electronics of anything it hits. We call it a Mag-Gun." Zach says beaming, extending it out so Frank can see it better. "Whatever electronic based item you fire at, the object catches the pulse which generates a rogue current of electricity. The current moves through the device's circuits and destroys them. No fuss, no muss."

"Let me guess." Franks says. "For the drones. A bit of overkill maybe?"

"Not with the ones we use, I mean they use." Zach answers correcting himself. "This new design of drone was developed by the Defense Department. They're modeled to look like a dragonfly and are the size of a large mouse. Very high tech and you need one of these to put them down."

"I get it. I pepper the teams with a few shots just to let them know we're here and as they send in the drones, you're going to take then out with that."

"Exactly. We can't rush it though. We need the drones follow us in a ways. Let them think that there's just the two of us. Whether they believe that or not, is another matter and I'll take the drones out when they've seen enough."

"How many do you think they have?" Frank asks.

"There is only one unit down there so it should be six drones max and they'll hold at least one back. I'm sure they know we have Mag-Guns." Before Zach can say more, a drone is hovering in the entranceway. He fires a few bursts and puts it down. "They're coming! We don't have much time!" He yells.

Frank leans against the cave entrance wall and can see team members starting to advance a half mile away. He braces the rifle against the wall and randomly fires peppering the ground around them and watches them scatter. Another drone enters the cave. Zach lets it advance a few yards before firing, sending it crashing to the floor. Frank back pedals, reloads another clip and continues firing, aiming at nothing. He grabs the duffle bag and starts to sprint into the cave. Zach grabs the other case as he holds the Mag-gun with one arm, watching for more drones, letting each one advance a little farther in before firing. Frank stops, lets Zach pass and he fires some more. Zach spots another and shoots, there's no escaping the EMP pulse and it spirals to the ground…four down, maybe two to go. They're about three hundred yards in when they hear the blast of concussion grenades echoing in the cave. They turn and run as fast as they can, not encountering a single Tsiatko as they proceed. As they turn a bend, Brother is waiting.

"Wait by the Orb." Brother orders as they pass. They slow to a trot, trusting Brother has their back.

"Montgomery," Ramsey calls out through his head set. What do you see?" He and his teams are just outside the cave and have just lobbed in the concussion grenades.

"Allmass has been taking out the drones as he retreats. It's just him and one other in there. No sign of any Tsiatko." Montgomery replies.

"Go, go, go," Ramsey orders his men.

The teams advance, activating their night vision goggles as they enter. They form lines on either side of the pathway with each member leaving six feet between them, their weapons at the ready as they advance. As the last of the eighty enter, they're completing a trail of soldiers two hundred and forty feet with those entering last facing backwards to protect the rear. They haven't encountered any resistance yet and the only sounds are of their boots on the wet and rocky cave floor. What they're not aware of is that they're entering a gauntlet. One that none has ever experienced before. Brother lets out a howl that rumbles and echoes through the cavern and Ramsey immediately holds up a clench fist which is mimicked along the line and the men stop. The moment they halt, powerful arms simultaneously reach out everywhere from within the cave walls clawing and grabbing at the team members and those unfortunate to be found by the Tsiatko's grip, are violently pulled in to the walls. Most of the team members have no chance to yell or scream in protest and those that didn't keep a death grip on their weapon, leave them to clatter to the cave floor. The handful that have laid witness to this and escaped the initial wrath, are panic king, shouting for their comrades while spinning in circles looking for their invisible predators. Tsiatko charge out from their concealment, shoving these remaining few into their rocky crypts, then it's done. The Tsiatko emerge, over a hundred strong, and let out a unified roar of victory. The sound carries deep into the cavern to where Frank and Zach are waiting by the Orb. The few Beings that were assigned to remain there with them roar back in response. The sound becomes deafening and the two men cover their ears for protection. They suspect what has just transpired and Frank involuntarily shivers, imagining his fate had Gaylord not had a firm hold of him.

Brother triumphantly struts his way to where the ambush has taken place. The few weapons left on the muddy pathway are the only evidence that these units that had tracked them down for so many years, were even here. But wait…there's one other corroboration, Ramsey's head is left exposed outside the cavern wall. His lifeless eyes still open wide, his face still expresses the shock and disbelief of the terror he'd just experienced. Ramsey will not have to be concerned about becoming a disposable asset no more. Brother peers down at it, gazing into those empty eyes for a moment before placing his large meaty hand over it and slowly pushes it into the rock, seemingly taking pleasure with every inch disappearing from his sight. With the harsh undertaking complete, he roars once more and his brethren join in his celebration. Their sounds of triumph are so loud and deafening, they escape from the tunnel as if they were being shouted through a megaphone to the lone drone unit remaining in the parking lot.

Montgomery pauses as the sounds reverberate against the Humvee. "Ramsey! Can you hear me?!" He shouts into his head set. There's no response. "Ramsey… any Team Leaders, respond!" There's only stillness. "Anyone! Someone! Respond!" He calls out desperately. He waits a few moments longer, listening to the unbearable silence. "How many drones do we have left?" He asks.

"Only one sir." A pilot says.

"Fuck! Send it in." He orders and watches the monitor as it approaches the cavern. "Take it slow and easy."

It hovers near the entrance and the pilot is constantly weaving it to try and avoid being a target. Cautiously it's piloted in, its sensors trying to capture any movement or images. As it reaches the scene of the ambush, the live feed picks up sight of a shotgun on the ground, there's nothing else. The pilot guides it forward and there's nothing more than the bare cave walls, a few footprints embedded in the mud and the odd weapon strewn about.

"Where are they?" Montgomery asks desperately.

The drone weaves side to side, up and down in constant flight as it continues onward, trying to reduce the risk of becoming the quarry of some unseen hunter.

Montgomery stands. His breathing is heavy and he's in a bit of a panic. "Where the fuck are they?!" He shouts. "Goddamn it... someone, please?" He pleads.

The drone continues bend after bend but there's no one. Finally a light is picked up in the distance.

"Yes!" Montgomery shouts relieved.

Frank is holding the Mag-Gun now. "Hold off." Zach says as the drone approaches. The drone stops and hovers. Frank looks at Zach. "Not yet." Zach says. He allows a few moments pass, "Now!"

Frank fires, the drone drops and Zach stomps on it.

"Son... of... a... bitch." The words slip slowly from Montgomery's lips. "We need to get this video to Belette, now!" He orders.

CHAPTER FOURTEEN

Bertram rushes into Felix Belette's office. "Sir, a Richard Montgomery has sent you a video feed from one of the drones at Rainier. He's demanded that I tell you it's imperative you view it immediately."

"What's the hell's going on there?"

"Sir, all I know is what I have been told." Bertram says as he approaches Felix's desk.

"Alright then, bring it up for me." Felix says as he pushes his chair back to give Bertram access to his computer.

After a few keystrokes, Bertram steps back so Felix has a clear view of the video on his monitor.

Felix puts it on pause. "Who sent this?" he asks.

"Richard Montgomery sir, apparently he heads the drone unit."

"Oh yes, Montgomery. Connect me with him so he can answer any questions I have watching this?" Felix says.

"Yes sir, give me a minute." Bertram dials a number on Felix's landline, a cell number he's written on his palm, and passes the handset to Belette.

"Montgomery here," Richard answers.

"Montgomery, Belette here, what's this you sent me?"

"A video taken from a drone after we lost communication with the teams."

"Lost contact? With all of them … how?"

"Sir," Richard says. "You need to watch the video."

"What about Ramsey?" Felix asks.

"Sir," Richard says louder, "Please … you need to see the video."

"Fine, I'll watch it but … I better get some answers." Felix demands.

"Sir, please, for the love of God … just view it." Richard begs.

Felix plays the video. He watches as the view moves forward into the cavern. It's eerie to see it through the eyes of the drone displayed in thermal and infrared imaging. The drone hovers over weapons discarded on the cave floor, some still showing warm grips on the stocks that come alive in an orange red glow, from the team members' hands. The scene continues on along the cold blue cave walls, turn after turn of empty space. Finally it reveals light from a distance source. As it approaches the origin of the illumination, the image displays lights bouncing off the cave walls from where the Orb rests. The video pans beyond to reveal the silhouettes of a mass of large indistinguishable figures that fill the entire cave background. As the pilot switches it from thermal to standard, it drops its view to show two others who are posed in front of these indistinct bodies. It is Allmass and Smirnov. Smirnov is holding a Mag-Gun; Allmass has a fist up with the middle finger raised in an act of defiance. There's movement from Smirnov and the screen goes dead. In his own way, Allmass has just told Belette to fuck off.

Felix reclines back in his chair, still holding the phone tight against his ear. "Any sign of the teams?'

"No sir." Montgomery replies.

Felix hangs up, says nothing, does nothing, just sits and stares. Finally, he leans forward, punching in a number and switches it to speaker phone as it rings.

"Yes." A man answers.

"Commander, this is Felix Belette. I need you to immediately dispatch a squadron of Apache Helicopters armed with Hellfire missiles to Mt. Rainier. A Richard Montgomery on site will provide the coordinates for an immediate strike there. We've lost several team members at that location and it's imperative we take immediate action." Felix demands.

"Who is this?" The Commander asks.

"Belette goddamn it … we don't have time! We have video evidence of a large number of hostiles that must immediately be taken out! You fire on every open cavern you can find! You hear me?!" Belette shouts.

"Belette, that's an active volcano! Do you have any concept of the potential collateral damage that could be inflicted on the local population?! Are you out of your friggin mind?!" The Commander harshly replies.

The conversation is interrupted by the appearance of Reggie in Belette's office. She's looking quite attractive in dark green crocodile leather heels, a Pantone palette Kale green dress that stops just above her knees, a large gold metallic necklace around her neck and her long red hair tied back in a pony tail. She calmly strolls towards his desk, ignoring his waves of protest.

"Reggie, damn it, I don't have the time right now!" He shouts as she nears.

"Your right Felix, you don't." She says as she raises her arm. She's holding a silencer equipped .22 caliber automatic and shoots Felix in the forehead. His head is propelled back hard against his brown, custom made leather office chair.

"Shit!" Bertram yelps as he jumps back.

Reggie continues around the desk and pumps two more in Felix's chest. She turns her attention to the phone. "Commander, cancel that directive."

"Who's this?" is his stern reply.

"This is Reggie Byrnes, the NEW AR for the Committee. The Committee decided it could not tolerate another Mt. St. Helens fiasco or anymore plane blunders so, with a little persuasion from me, Mr. Belette has elected to take… an early retirement." She says as she views Belette's lifeless corpse. She glances at Bertram. "Just breath, relax." She whispers. She gives her attention back to the Commander. "Now Commander, you do have a choice. You can question my authority, but if you do, I WILL serve your… genitals on a platter." She states calmly. "Ignore the directive Belette gave you, forget you ever heard it. Am I making myself clear?" She demands.

There's a slight pause. "Yes ma'am."

"Thank you." She says and ends the call. She heads for the door, the firearm swinging to and fro at her side. "Bertram," She calls out as she walks, "Get some help in here and clean up this mess. I have my interior designer coming tomorrow and I want it to look presentable." She stops as she opens the door and looks back at him, still standing in place by the desk. "And get all those paintings into storage too?"

"Yes ma'am."

"Oh, before I forget, send me Montgomery's number right away."

CHAPTER FIFTEEN

"I hate to say this," Oin says bursting in, "We may have a problem. There's a shitload of military at Rainier and the Sherriff's Department has the entire park cordoned off." He says.

"And Frank?" Willow asks.

"Haven't a clue." Oin says.

"Now what?" Stogie Man asks.

Willow props her elbows on her station, clasps her hands and rests her forehead on this human version of a pyramid. She sits in silence, deep in thought, contemplating their options as Oin and Stogie Man patiently wait. She looks up, parting her arms in quiet exasperation as she leans back. "For the moment, nothing, we do nothing, I need to think things through again." She says. "I want to make sure we're doing this right."

"Why re-examine it all?" Oin asks.

Willow shakes her head in uncertainty, "Why? Because we're considered renegades for disobeying the directive of abandoning this colonization and we have no outside support, it's just us. I need a moment to rethink this through." Sure, there were other teams of Handlers that felt the same way, ones that thought and talked about doing what Willow, Oin and Stogie Man did, but they were the only ones to act on it. "I just don't want to regret anything by rushing." Willow says.

"We get that but consider where we'll stand if this pans out." Stogie Man says smiling.

"Our initial responsibility was only to nudge things along and hopefully let them," as Willow points outward, "Make the right decision. With the parameters we were given, we knew we couldn't control everything, we never could and we weren't meant to, just nudge things along but now, flying by the seat of our pants…I don't know. I know we're finally at a juncture now where everything lies with a specific group of individuals and I need to make sure I, we, have all the bases covered." Willow adds.

"We've did a hell a lot of damage with our nudging." Stogie Man says. "We sacrificed a lot of people, following those damn guidelines we were forced to adhere to. With each colonization, we achieved no better results than the first so, like you said, we need to attack this from a different perspective if we're going to get anywhere. We're doing it your way now."

"We know you're right Willow. The fault with these experiments was letting the population make all the critical decisions once we've done our…thing." Oin says.

"I so much wanted to have faith in everything we did, faith in this process, faith in humankind and faith in…shit, I don't know anymore." She answers.

"Why are we re-hashing all this? Willow," Stogie Man says. "Our point is we trust you on this. We're not out to second guess you; we just want to understand your game plan." Stogie Man stands; shaking his head slightly as he paces and turns to them his arms extended his palms up. "We understand the key to actually achieve the success we've chased for so long is NOT to follow the text book…so why so hesitant to share your entire plan with us?"

"Because I still question what I'm doing but I keep asking myself, what are the alternatives?" Willow says. "I know what the end result will be otherwise." She's also worried about getting too close; nothing personal that would complicate the future decisions she has to make. That's what she fears with Frank. Will she let emotions get in the way of what must be done? But she doesn't share that with her partners.

"Look, we're all sick and tired of everything ending in disaster each time. Sick and tired of the death and destruction that goes with this job. It's time for a change Willow, that's why we're here with you, for you." Oin says. "Who are you still trying to convince because we sure as hell don't need any?"

"You may not like where I'm going with all this?" Willow warns.

"Enough with the talk, just tell us what's next?" Stogie Man asks without hesitation.

Willow stands. "We crank things up another level and we start with Frank and Allmass and then…the Committee." She says.

"Yes." Oin hisses pumping his fist to the floor.

Stogie Man nods his endorsement.

CHAPTER SIXTEEN

"Montgomery?" Reggie clarifies over the phone.

"Yes. Who is this?" He asks.

"This is Reggie Byrnes. I'm Felix Belette's replacement."

"Oh." Montgomery answers, "When did this all happen?"

"Mr. Belette needed to take an immediate leave of absence, serious health issues I'm told. The stress was, killing him." She states smiling.

"Sorry to hear that ma'am … uh, I meant about Belette, not you ma'am."

"I'm sure you did." She says slyly. "In regards to the situation at Rainier, I need you to immediately destroy all the video evidence, everything. Understand me?" She states.

"Ma'am?"

"Montgomery, I trust I don't have to repeat myself?"

"Uh, no ma'am."

"I had hoped not."

"Yes, ma'am, I mean no ma'am to having to repeat yourself, ma'am." Montgomery blubbers.

Reggie shakes her head, quietly giggling, entertained by his reaction.

"And the rest of the … situation?" Montgomery asks.

"Here is how it's going to play out. I have advised the Sherriff's Department that the teams encountered a large toxic gas pocket and all were lost including the terrorist suspect." Reggie states.

"I understand." Montgomery says.

"Yes, unfortunately Ramsey didn't have the forethought to equip themselves with gas monitors. Such a terrible loss of life isn't it?" She asks.

"Yes ma'am, terrible."

"The Sherriff's Department has been instructed to use their men to transport all the teams' vehicles to their secure lot for temporary storage. I trust you and your men can handle packing up the tent and any other equipment left scattered around for the Sherriff?"

"You can ma'am."

"I have deployed a four man security team with the directive to secure the cavern entrance until our recovery team can arrive to remove the remains. The security team should be on site within an hour or two. You do understand that appearances must be maintained?" Reggie asks.

"I do ma'am, but…"

"But what?"

"No disrespect, but that doesn't leave us much protection?'

"Not that you or anyone should be questioning my judgment but the teams demise was because of the stupid irrational decision to attack. The Tsiatko were defending themselves and, to be honest, the teams got what they deserved. So no, you won't have much protection because you aren't going to need it. They aren't looking for war. Can I continue now or do you want to question me more Montgomery?" Reggie says, her tone far from pleasant.

"No ma'am."

"Good, the recovery team and their transport vehicles are scheduled to arrive in the morning. They'll feign the loading and transfer of the teams' bodies. When their performance is done, they've been instructed to seal the entrance up tight. Can you overnight at that location so that you can assist if required?"

"Definitely ma'am, we can."

"And finally, the Sherriff's Department has been instructed that their participation is only required for the vehicle transport, nothing else, due to the sensitivity of the matter. He's also been directed that if anyone in his department speaks or permits any media access, the full wrath of the NSA and its associated agencies will be upon him. The Sherriff has assured me his full cooperation." She says. "Just so you know, not that it matters but our people in the FAA have already lifted the air zone restriction and will advise those that may inquire, that the temporary ban was a false alarm."

"I understand ma'am, anything else?" Montgomery asks.

"Actually there is and this is very important. When all is said and done, you and your men leave and forget about today. Can you and your men do that Montgomery or is there going to be a problem? I don't like problems." Reggie states.

"No ma'am, no problem but I do need a clarification."

"And what would that be?" She asks.

"We were assigned to assist these teams to hunt the Tsiatko. Where will the replacements units be based so I know where we're supposed to go?"

"Oops." Reggie says coyly, "I should have mentioned this, that particular program is discontinued. No teams means, no project. The resources and costs aren't justified. It' not like they had huge success. So, I am going to be nice and ALLOW your group to quit. Find something in the private sector and all of you will be provided a generous retirement package. Oh, unless you have an issue with that? Do you Montgomery? Want to question me on that as well?" She asks.

"No ma'am."

"Didn't think so, and by the way, you and your men will need to find a ride, take a bus, hitchhike, whatever you need to do tomorrow but your Humvee stays with the rest of the vehicles." She says hanging up.

Montgomery had heard of Belette's reputation but nothing compares to this woman. She scares the crap out of him. "Bitch," He mutters as he pockets his phone. "Okay men, pack up your personal things cause everything else stays, looks like tomorrow we might be walking from here."

"What you mean walking?" One of them asks.

"I'll explain later. Like it or not, we've got work to do first." Montgomery replies. He has a big decision to make in the morning…face the drudgery of walking to Ashton or tolerate an endless stream of questions from the deputies if they ask for a ride.

Reggie takes a seat at her desk and plays the video Montgomery had sent. She freezes on the frame which shows the Orb, Allmass, and Smirnov with their accomplices in the background. Interesting allegiances. Upon her disposable of Felix, she had the forethought to immediately provide the Committee a detailed summary of the recent events. Although the AR position includes a large portfolio of responsibilities, upon their review they had no issue with granting her request of four weeks to concentrate on the situation at hand. Her other obligations were delegated accordingly. "This is going to be fun." She says out loud, taking a sip of Perrier from her glass. "What to do, what to do, what to do?" As she taps a manicured nail against the glass.

"Allmass, you're a sly son of a bitch." She says to the images on the screen. "And Smirnov, I need to get to know you better. Get inside your head. Yes, I, do." She was already privy to the fact the Tsiatko had the Orb and for quite some time, years actually. If this Orb was suppose to be their salvation, why haven't they done anything with it? What're they waiting for? It's sitting there in plain sight. She takes another sip before getting up to get Triscuits and humus from her mini fridge. Eating helps her think. She sits back down as she munches. Something has to tie everyone in. What? If Allmass found out everything about Mr. H and how the Orb was the Tsiatko's saving grace at the castle… wouldn't Smirnov know everything too? He found the castle first… and she doubts Allmass reported about everything he found. So if Smirnov is alive, Allmass didn't shoot him. So who shot Allmass's associates? Allmass had to have. He wouldn't have permitted Smirnov to, and then just let him walk; it had to be the other way around. Allmass shot them to cover up he let Smirnov go. What did Smirnov have or know that Allmass found so important? It had to be more than school mates or friends. You don't kill two associates for someone you hung around with, what, forty five plus years ago? Then again, if Smirnov had something so important, why would Allmass try and kill him later in Belize? That part doesn't make sense either. And why didn't Smirnov kill Allmass in retaliation in San Francisco? And why pair up to get to the Orb and end up joining with creatures that have never have had any recorded association with man or openly harm them, well, except for the teams but the reasons there are obvious but why not Allmass, he headed up those teams? She stares at the picture on her monitor. So why? Why, would the Tsiatko allow him to be there? They had to have known about Allmass if they attacked the team at Trinity Alps? None of this makes sense. What's she missing? She empties her glass, walks to refill it and trades the humus and biscuits for trail mix. She plops back down in her chair. What could everyone have in common? It has to be there, staring her right in the face. Reggie had moved everything from her and Felix's meeting in the conference room, to her office after they were done. She moves to the work table and corkboard. Felix first got his rep back in Mr. H's day when he blew up the Solomons' lab. They were geneticists, rumoured to be working on a cloning project, trying to duplicate what the Handlers did to re-generate themselves. She looks for what she has on the Solomons and finds a write up on them. They were geneticists, known for dabbling in new theoretical directions. Makes sense but hang on; they both have degrees in Zoology too. Why would Mr. H need that qualification if they're cloning humans even if you take in consideration the anomalies the Committee is eliminating? Neanderthals are still humans relatively speaking? Wait a minute. If Mr. H was responsible for dissecting and analyzing the Tsiatko, he would've had all kinds of genetic samples. The Solomons were both geneticists AND zoologists and were involved in the field of embryo modification, something that was virtually unknown in their time. She stops and looks at her monitor, slowly creeping toward it staring at the screen. "No way." As she stops to focus on Smirnov. Smirnov had no birth certificate. She couldn't figure out where he came from before he lived with his grandparents. "This can't be… but it would make sense of everything though." She says to no one. She drops in her chair and touches Smirnov's face on the screen. "I need to recheck the year the Solomons died." Reggie goes back through the documents and confirms the year. Her theory has merit. Is this what Felix was trying to hide when he blew up their lab? He had to have the Committee's approval which would mean they're holding things back on her. Huh, no one trusts anyone. Well, she doesn't either so tit for tat. She'll be holding a few things back too. But how does she prove her theory, how? She picks up the phone and punches in a number.

"Sherriff Barton here."

"Sherriff, its Reggie Byrnes." She says, back to playing the role of a senior NSA member.

"Ms. Byrnes, I can absolutely assure you the Ashford Sherriff's Department has followed your directives to a tee and there's absolutely."

"Sherriff." She interrupts. "I have complete faith in your abilities. I'm calling about another matter."

"Oh… alright, what would that be?"

"It's in regards to your Deputy Frank Smirnov."

"Really? I'm a bit surprised by that."

"Sherriff, I acknowledge we're a large agency with a high volume of highly sensitive cases but we do care about our fellow members in law enforcement."

"Well, I do appreciate that ma'am and we welcome your involvement in his case."

"Are there are personal items of Deputy Smirnov remaining?"

"Yes, of course. All of them."

"What do you mean by all of them?" Reggie asks.

"Everything. We sealed up his entire house. Didn't remove a thing after we went through it. We couldn't locate any next of kin and as he's only considered a missing person, we had no authority or reason to do otherwise."

Reggie looks upward and mouths the words thank you. "Sherriff, not that I doubt the capabilities of your local office but I'm sending down a forensic team to go through Smirnov's place. As you're aware, our terrorist suspect was a person of interest in his disappearance and we want to make sure nothing was overlooked."

"Absolutely, as I said, I welcome any help you can provide on this."

"Great. My team will be there tomorrow and they'll contact you upon their arrival."

"Yes, ma'am."

Reggie disconnects the call and brings the image from the cavern back up. "Gotcha." She says, sitting back and smiling.

CHAPTER SEVENTEEN

The Tsiatko are milling around the cavern like it's a social event and there's a welcome difference in the Tsiatko's attitude toward Zach. He's now considered a brother in arms and is constantly rewarded with slaps on the back, so much so it's getting painful and he has to back away from the physical contact without trying to be unreceptive to their rejoicing.

"I bet you never expected this?" Frank asks.

"Never in my wildest dreams." Zach says, "And it's a fuckin relief."

They take a seat on the rocks and gaze at the Orb.

"Now what?' Zach asks.

"You know, there's something off about the Tsiatko and the Orb. It still bothers me that they've had it for so long and, if it's the key to their salvation, why haven't they done anything with it?" Frank says in a hushed voice. Frank would like to tell Zach about the note in the pouch but he can't. Regardless what the two of them have been through, Mr. H's message was clear, don't trust anyone. And considering the weight he has on his shoulders, the one supposedly responsible for the continued survival of mankind, he's heeding Mr. H's warnings. "Have you noticed there's a circle of stones around it now and I've been watching, even with the crowd in here, the Tsiatko make a deliberate effort of not getting too close. Like it's the plague."

"I hear you. I remember when we first got here and Brother refused to touch it. He got quite irritated when I pushed the matter." Zach whispers.

"That didn't slip by me either." Frank states quietly.

"So if it's no value to them, why don't they let us have it?"

"And what are we going to do with it? We really don't know shit about it. We can't just mess with it. As far as we know if we screw with it too much, the damn thing will go off and blow us to smithereens." Frank whispers, that feeling of mistrust is re-surfacing.

Zach senses this and he needs to maintain Frank's faith. He decides to open up a bit to get him back on his side. "Frank, view things from my perspective. This planet is hell in a handbag. It's done and in my opinion, we can't change shit. And now, I've lost any place I may have had with the Committee if they're successful in relocating. The Orb is the only thing that may save my ass. How? I haven't a fucking clue but its better than anything I have going right now. Maybe you have some wild idea you can save the world. Me, I don't see how you can. Christ, look around. How're you going to fight these things if it comes to that? We probably saw just a fragment of what they can do. The only way we could take them on is to nuke them… and in the process we nuke ourselves. There's be no escaping the fallout and, if we did, what kind of world would we be living in?" Zach says exasperated.

Frank scans around, still cautious of prying ears but it appears they're still being ignored. He gets what Zach is saying. He doesn't know himself how he's suppose to accomplish his pre-destined task. Maybe it's just a pipe dream. He decides to change the subject. "So what do you think Belette's going to do now?"

Zach takes a breath before replying. He knows Franks intent with that question. "I'm at a bit of a loss on that. His teams are gone. I'm not sure how the Committee is going to react to that?" Zach says.

"I'd hate to be in his shoes. Whatever he gets, he deserves it." Frank says.

"I agree." Zach replies. "Okay then, if we're changing subjects, what's the story with Oin and the other two in the SUV?"

Frank briefly explains how he met Oin and Willow, his constant sightings of Stogie Man and his surprise of suddenly seeing them altogether in the parking lot.

"Who do you think they are?" Zach asks.

"I haven't any idea but my gut tells me they're nothing I have to be worried about. In fact just the opposite, like they've been helping me out. Doesn't make any sense." He raises his arms in the air and looks around again, "But what part of any of this makes any sense."

Zach stands and nods to Frank to follow. "Why don't we go have a look at what's happening outside? We could use the air."

Frank gets up and looks around. "Sure." They only venture a few yards before Gaylord stops them.

"What's up big guy?" Zach asks.

"You cannot go out there. There are armed men at the entrance." Gaylord says.

"Are they planning another assault?" Frank asks concerned.

Brother approaches from behind. "No, I believe not. There are only two of them. It would seem they are there to prevent any from entering. We will let them be." He says. He looks back at the other Tsiatko. "It has been a glorious day for us but it has taken a toll. It will be a night of rest. We ALL have earned it." Patting Frank on the shoulder before leaving them, Gaylord follows him.

Frank now realizes they don't have as much free reign as they'd hoped. Obviously, whatever they do next they'll still need Brother's approval. Another night then. Frank looks at Zach and he can see that neither of them are going to tolerate being cooped up in this cave much longer.

Suddenly Zach scampers after Brother. "Brother," He calls out, "Our weapons and equipment can't be left out in the dampness of this cavern so we must move them into one of our tents. I just wanted to let you know in case your question our motives."

Brother looks to Frank and then back at Zach. "You do what you think is best with them. I believe your intentions are true and   I thank you for telling me. It does further ease my distrust in you." And Brother continues on.

"Really, what kind of bullshit is that?" Frank asks. "Not how I wanted to end the day."

"Believe me. You'll thank me later." Zach whispers smiling.

"Christ… I know that look and I don't like it." Frank mutters.

"You will." Zach whispers excitedly.

It's a laborious task, not so much the duffle bags, it's the ammo boxes. They seem to weigh a ton but they struggle their way into the tent with them and let them drop. They each use them for seats.

"Ok." Frank whispers, shaking his head. "What do you have up your sleeve?"

"Do you want out of here or not?"

"Yea, but I don't know if I want to know how." Frank says quietly, dreading what he's about to hear.

Zach gets up and moves to the tent floor, motioning Frank to do the same. Zach unlatches one of the ammo boxes and tosses Frank a large box. He reads the label, "CR 12 Gauge Tear Gas Explosive Projectiles."

"You thought we would need these against the teams?" Frank quietly asks.

"No, against them." Zach says, thumbing outside. "I'd say they shouldn't trust me any farther than they could throw me but, I think they can toss me pretty far." He chuckles.

"CR?" That's crazy stuff." Frank says.

"Yea, ten times stronger than riot squads would use. One thing I do know about the Tsiatko is their eyes and their lungs are the same as us. This stuff causes temporary blindness and severely affects the breathing and causes immediate incapacitation."

"But isn't it toxic in confined spaces?"

"Yea, that's the down side but I'm sure the Tsiatko are as tough as they think they are and will survive. The up side is, if this works, they may hesitate before acting next time … give us an advantage down the road."

"What about us?" Frank asks.

Zach reaches over to a duffle bag and removes a complicated looking helmet and hands it to Frank. "That my friend is an Integrated Ballistic Helmet. Lightweight, full communication capability, hearing protection, night vision and gas mask all rolled up into one."

"Weren't you worried about the Tsiatko checking?"

"Why would they plus they wouldn't have a clue about this stuff." Zach says. "I don't know about you but I wasn't planning on staying here any longer than I had to."

"So … were you thinking of using this solo and grabbing the Orb for yourself?" Frank asks.

"Um … the thought did cross my mind." Zach admits.

"What changed it?"

"You. I believe that for whatever reason, you're more important to them than the Orb. I don't know why but that's the only thing that makes sense. Why else just leave the Orb in that shrine since the time Mr. H gave it to them? Why welcome you in like they have? They've got an agenda of their own and you're a big part of it, whatever it is. Plus you said yourself you don't trust them."

Frank isn't sure how to reply. Unsure what the answers are. "You're prepared to leave the Orb behind?" He asks pessimistically.

"For now. I don't think it's going anywhere soon."

"I hope this doesn't come back to bite me in the ass but I agree, we need to get out of here and you're right, I don't think they'll hurt me. For some reason, they need me." Frank says. He turns to crawl to the tent door.

"Where're you going?" Zach asks.

"For a smoke, I need to think things through."

"What do you mean a smoke?"

Frank reaches inside his shirt and draws out a plastic bag. "I stole Oin's weed and papers." He says laughing. "Want to join me?"

"No, I'll pass. Just hurry up and let's just get this over with okay?"

"Yea, yea." Frank replies.

Frank exits to an apparently empty cavern but he knows because it appears that way, doesn't mean it is nor does he care at this stage and takes a seat by the Orb. He rolls a joint, lights it and inhales deeply. He feels a sense of calm envelope him by the time he exhales. He stares at the Orb wandering what secrets lies within it. A lot of people have died over it and he hopes he'll eventually find out if it was worth it. He senses motion and turns to see Brother walk in. "Taking a break." He says holding up the joint. "Marijuana…weed, it helps me relax and think."

"I am familiar with the scent. Your kind has been using it for centuries. It has a pleasant smell." Brother says. "Gaylord, has you have named him, told me of his enjoyment partaking in your ritual. You are preparing for battle?"

"Uh?" Frank says a bit taken back by the question before it hits home. "No, no that was just my friend's way of getting him to smoke it, a bit of trickery. I do this to help me view the world from a different perspective. Nothing more."

"I understand." Brother says with a slight grin.

"Brother." Frank says. "You must…have faith in me."

Brother is the one now taken back by Frank's words. "You have not failed us?"

"No, but I fear my actions one day will…disappoint you."

"Have no fear my brethren." As he turns and walks away. "Have no fear." He calls back. "You will do what you know is right."

Frank's not sure if that's the answer of atonement he was hoping for or whether he's looking for any at all. He takes another healthy drag wishing for the old days when he just didn't give a shit.

CHAPTER EIGHTEEN

"Remember, whatever you do, stay in the middle of the cavern. We don't know if any that may be in the walls, will be affected." Frank says.

"What the fuck? I'm stupid now and have been oblivious to everything?" Zach replies, a bit annoyed.

"Sorry, not use to having someone along. Still thinking I'm dealing with a rookie." Franks says smiling.

They're loaded down pretty good. They each have Kevlar vests under their shirts and two Glocks in the back of their waistbands with several spare clips tucked in the side pockets of their khaki pants. Frank has a shotgun cross slung over each shoulder, one loaded with CR tear gas and the other with live rounds. Zach has two as well, one with CR and the other with bean bag rounds in hope of taking out the guards at the entrance without killing them. They've reduced the contents of their backpacks to a minimum and have them on facing front with the zippered top pouches filled with assorted shotgun rounds.

"When we leave the tent, you fire a couple rounds to the back and I'll fire a couple forward, one short and one long. From there we bee line for the exit and do the same as we go, one short one long. We reload as we go; continual shots." Frank says. The tear gas rounds can travel up to three hundred feet.

Zach gives Frank the what am I stupid look, again. "And when we hit the entrance, I'll take out the guards. I got it, I got it." Zach replies.

They put on the Ballistic Helmets, adjusting the fit and activate the communications.

"Can you hear me?" Zach asks.

"Loud and clear, ready?"

"Let's do this." Zach says.

They exit, firing as they'd planned. They cavern fills with a thick misty smoke that becomes denser with each round. As they sprint past the Orb, Zach has second thoughts for a millisecond about his decision but keeps running. They motor their way through, scanning the walls as they progress but the tear gas restricts their vision. The air in the mask has an unpleasant rubbery sanitized smell. It also takes a moment for their eyes to adjust to the changing view as the tear gas creates an eerie glow with the night vision goggles and the heat from it adds a reddish tinge. They keep scanning back but can't see or hear anything in pursuit and after twenty minutes of moving at a hard pace, they slow down as they can see the exit in the distance.

"Ready?" Frank asks.

"Ready." Zach replies as he switches shotguns in preparation to take out the guards. They're expecting strong resistance even if there is just two posted at the entrance.

Frank turns to face the cavern interior, watching the rear. The tear gas is slowly flowing past him, drawn outward by the fresh air and they hope it has an effect on the sentries, disorientates them or at least masks their approach. He looks back as Zach creeps out of the cavern, hugging the wall as best he can for additional cover. Zach advances thirty feet, suddenly shielding his eyes while continually scanning from side to side for a hint of the guards' location.

"Clear." Zach calls back.

Frank proceeds out cautiously and realizes why Zach was protecting his eyes. Frank has to do the same as the moon is out, full and bright, irritating his eyes through the night vision lenses and he switches them it off but leaves his helmet in place as the mist of irritants is still escaping the cavern. They crouch and take cover at the end of the arms of debris that the Tsiatko had cleared. "Where are they?" Franks asks.

"No idea." Zach replies.

"Let's get farther down; I need to get this damn helmet off." Frank says.

They move at a faster pace, splitting out and wide, stopping after twenty-five yards to survey the area. The moon lights up everything as it reflects off the thin cover of snow on the ground. Nothing, they advance again, same distance. Frank takes off his helmet and clips its strap on a belt loop. Zach does the same, moving out farther as he does. Frank looks back and spots Brother and Gaylord standing at the entrance, the mist exiting and flowing out around their bodies. They seem unaffected by it. Frank becomes oblivious to the potential dangers and stands to watch them. Gaylord takes a step forward but Brother extends an arm stopping him, shaking his head no... Gaylord could have caught up with him in moments, instead Gaylord and Brother turn to go back in but Brother pauses to look back once more before continuing. Frank suddenly feels a sense of sadness and heartache, something he's not use to experiencing and he's torn about what he's just done. He's bombarded with self-doubts. Did they let them go, why? And if so, why not just let them walk out rather than "escape"? Why the theatrics? Were they for Zach's benefit, part of the bigger plan?

"Frank." Zach calls out as he comes running up. "What're you doing? We need to keep going. What is it?" Zach looks up at the entrance where Frank is staring but there's nothing to see.

Frank turns to him. "Nothing... just checking, let's go. Did you spot anyone?"

"Nothing. Where are they?" Zach asks referring to the guards.

Frank shrugs and can't help but glance back once more, wondering if Brother and Gaylord may still be watching from the dark of the entranceway. They move towards the lot, keeping low as they know there has to be other support personnel on site. They're nearing the band of trees sheltering the parking area when three figures emerge, dressed in black, wearing ski masks. Zach's ready to fire a bean bag round but Frank pushes his barrel downward. "Hold up." Frank says as there's something strangely familiar about this group. The trio stops, removing their masks in turn before approaching further with the last one shoving an unlit cigar in his mouth upon his reveal. It's Willow, Oin and Stogie Man.

Frank stands his ground. "What the hell is this?" Frank demands.

"We were coming to help?" Oin says smiling.

"Hi." Willow says.

Stogie Man just nods.

"Leave your wife at home for this one?" Frank asks Stogie Man.

"Wife? Oh, yeah... she left me. She had enough of my complaints about her picture taking and ran off with her hairdresser." He laughs.

"I thought she would have had her fill of that crud hanging out of your mouth." Frank says.

Stogie Man takes the cigar from his mouth and carefully examines it before answering. "This is the reward of my labors." He chuckles.

Frank notices the unfamiliar weapons in their hands. "What are those?" He asks.

"These?" Willow says as she moves it nonchalantly. "Call them, high tech Taser guns."

"I guess you can talk after all." Franks says to her.

"I need the right motivation." She replies.

Zach elects to quietly listen to the exchange.

"Anyone else here?" Frank asks.

"Yea." Stogie Man pipes up chomping on the half smoked cigar, "But we took care of them."

"We had just taken out the guards by the cave when the tear gas starting rolling out so we dragged them down to the lot and were just coming back." Oin pipes in.

"Just the three of you?" Zach asks.

"We're not rookies, we've been watching for awhile and saw there were only a few left behind so we decided to tuck them away and try to find you." Willow says.

"A few?" Frank says.

"There were two more armed guys warming up in a vehicle but we took them down no problem. And the drone guys wasn't too enthusiastic about resisting." Stogie Man says smiling.

"We've got them all duct taped in a Humvee down there." Oin says laughing.

"Thanks, but why? Who are you working for?" Frank asks.

"Let's just get out of here first." Willow speaks up. "We can deal with the questions later." They move out and Frank and Zach feel that they have no choice but to follow. As they trot through the lot, Willow shouts back, "We're parked just off the highway about a quarter mile down."

They don't encounter anyone on the road and as they arrive at the same black SUV the group was in earlier, Stogie Man pops open the rear hatch. "You can throw your gear in here." He says before getting in the driver's seat and firing it up as Willow climbs in the front passenger side. Once they have their things in, Oin slams the hatch closed, the three of them get in the back seat with Oin in the middle and they drive off.

"Long time no see." Oin says beaming.

Frank and Zach ignore him, still unsure of this trio's intentions or where they're being taken. They've kept their Glocks tucked into their waistbands as a precaution. Stogie Man and Willow stare silently ahead as they drive.

"Where're we going?" Frank finally asks.

"It's not far. We'll be there soon." Willow says.

A few minutes later they turn off to a secondary highway and shortly after, they pull into the Miskata Lodge, they've only travelled ten miles. It's a high end place. Frank had driven by it many a time when he was working in this area but never stopped in.

"You're hiding here?" Zach asks.

"Who's hiding? We've got no one looking for us." Willow says, looking back smiling as Stogie Man parks. "You may as well leave your stuff in the back but… that's up to you. You can trust us or bring them up."

Zach and Frank hesitate but climb out along with everyone else leaving their stowed weapons in the back. They follow them in through a side entrance, grab the stairs to the second floor and head down the hallway. Oin swipes the electronic lock of a room and enters, they all follow.

"This is my room, consider it yours now," Oin says, tossing the key card on the coffee table. "I'll bunk with him." Indicating Stogie Man, "The bedroom is at the back and there are two queen beds, no sharing." Oin laughs.

"We have rooms on either side of this one." Willow says. "So if you do need anything, just knock on any one of the adjoining doors. I'm the one on the right. Make yourself at home, order whatever you want and charge it to the room."

"Pretty luxurious, you must have quite the allowance?" Zach says prodding for information.

Willow smiles in response. "We spend a lot of time working together, too much, so we take advantage of privacy whenever we can." She says. "Look," As she takes a seat on the arm of a leather chair, "We could play the cat and mouse game with questions all night but I'm sure you guys are tired. I know I am. Let's call it a night. We've got your back so rest, relax and tomorrow I'll answer your questions as best I can."

The events of the last few days are catching up with Frank. "Why not…honestly, I'm too tired to argue." He says. He's dragging his butt and has been running on fumes. "Zach, you good with this?"

"I am if you are…they're your fairy godmothers."

CHAPTER NIINETEEN

It's been a busy day for Reggie and she's in Felix's old office, her new digs, with an interior designer when Bertram knocks and enters.

"Ma'am. There's an urgent call for you on the landline." Bertram says.

"Wait outside for me please, I'll need some privacy." She says to the designer. "Bertram put the call through."

Bertram escorts the designer out as Reggie makes her way to the desk. Momentarily the phone beeps.

"Yes?" She answers.

"Ms. Byrnes, this is Sergeant Leland with the recovery team at Rainier."

"Yes Sergeant, what is it?"

"When we arrived on site, we found all the personnel bound and gagged in a Humvee."

"I have to believe alive then?"

"Yes ma'am."

"Where they able to identify anyone?"

"No ma'am. They were tasered by two, possibly three individuals dressed in black and wearing ski masks."

"Could they provide anything else? Vehicle?"

"No ma'am."

"Alright, finish what you were tasked to do, make sure everything is wrapped up there and let's get this over with."

"Yes ma'am."

She ends the call. Tasered. There was no listing of Tasers missing in the inventory from Seattle but that doesn't mean anything. Allmass and Zach? Maybe the three unidentified in the SUV? She knows they wouldn't have any satellite shots to help as she had to direct one specifically to that location last time. So what does it mean? Someone getting in or someone getting out?

Bertram steps in. "Sorry Ms. Byrnes but I saw you were done and I have another call on hold, a Ms. Sheppard from the forensic team in Ashford. She has an update for you."

"Put her through."

"Right away ma'am."

"Yes." Reggie says as she picks up the call.

"Ms. Byrnes, its Angela Sheppard. We're done here and we were able to recover enough suitable DNA samples for a profile."

"Perfect, how soon will you have it done?"

"With travel, we can have it in six hours. If we come across anything unexpected and need to do a re-analysis, add another four."

"I want to be very specific about this, you and only you will handle the samples for testing. You and only you will complete the testing and no one, no one is to have access at any time to the results. I'm giving you eight hours including any re-testing." Reggie says as she's confident Angela is going to come up with something peculiar.

"Yes ma'am, that's pushing the edge but I'll do it." Angela says hesitantly.

Reggie ends the call and takes a seat in Felix's cleaned chair, taking a moment. She wiggles in it trying to get comfortable , not concerned at all about it being the place where Belette met his demise. She can't wait to have something more her style in this space, oh, the decorator. She hits Bertram's extension.

"Yes." He answers.

"Ask the designer if she needs anything more?"

"One moment … she says no."

"Okay, thank her for her time and let her know she can schedule an appointment through you when she has something put together."

"Yes ma'am. Anything else?"

"No, that's it for now." Reggie says hanging up. She'd love to chase a lead on the three from the first satellite images of the SUV but she knows there's nothing there of value. There are a million SUVs and they have no specific description of it and trying to look for three people traveling together would be an endless task, they could have split up, be anywhere. She has to hope they get a hit from the facial recognition from the ATM pictures. She looks at her watch, he should have something by now, he's had it long enough and calls a number on her cell.

"Hello." A man answers.

"Sam, it's Reggie." They're work has intertwined for a couple of years and are on a first name basis.

"Hey boss! Look at you moving up in the world." Sam remarks.

"Yea, yea." She smiles. "Tell me you got something."

"Well, actually I did get a couple hits but … they don't make sense, its driving me nuts so I've been going through the software trying to find any glitches."

"What do you mean?"

"Hang on a sec." Sam says.

Reggie hears movement over the phone.

"You near a computer?" he asks.

"I'm at my desk."

"Ok … give me a moment here … okay, I sent you a couple images. Let me know when you have them and we can talk while you're looking at them."

Reggie opens her email, Sam's is there and she opens the attachment. "Got them." She says.

"Ok, besides all the law enforcement data bases, border security, yada, yada, yada." Sam says, "There are … bear with me a moment, ones that include artwork and photographs from hundreds of museums and archives worldwide. So … if you look at what I sent you, this is where I got a match on what you gave me."

"What am I looking at?" Reggie says.

"Well, the first one is an oil painting of Johannes Gutenberg."

"The guy who came up with the printing press."

"Very good, I'm impressed." Sam says.

"Thank you. See? Just not good looks." She says jokingly.

"Never thought you were, never thought you were." Sam says. "Have a look at the young man in the background of his workshop? See him?"

Reggie enlarges the image and peers at the screen. "Yea."

"Well, according to the software, he's a match. This painting is from the fourteen seventies, over five hundred and forty years ago."

"How?" Reggie asks.

"Well, there's slight room for error but this software is pretty sophisticated that's why I was looking for a glitch."

"And this other?"

"Well it's a photograph of Nikola Tesla taken in a public park in Budapest in eighteen hundred and eighty-one."

"The same year he came up with the Alternating-Current Electrical System, AC."

"The lady wins again!" Sam says. "Still the predominate electrical system we use today. Now… have a look at the guy behind him, off to the side with his hands in his pockets, leaning against the tree."

"It looks like the same person? How's that possible?" Reggie asks.

"It's not, it's impossible. Even though they're at different ages in these images, one a little younger and the other older, the program still scales them as a high percentile match, ninety-nine point two. That's why I was going through all the software again."

Reggie is in disbelief. She knows how it's plausible. "Thanks Sam, I'll leave this with you and let me know if anything comes up that'll make sense of it all."

"You got it boss, later." Sam says ending the call.

It's hard to fathom but, the three driving the SUV… have to be Handlers. They're supposed to be long gone? She needs the final piece of the puzzle which is Frank's DNA profile to confirm her suspicions and come up with a game plan.

She dials Bertram.

"Yes Ms. Byrnes?"

"Have the corkboard along with the table with all my research from my old office brought in here… and have Garth Scott come see me as well." She says. No matter what she does to kill the time, it's going to be a long eight hours to wait for the DNA profile.

CHAPTER TWENTY

"Morning sleepy head." Willow calls out.

Frank barely hears the words and can hardly open his eyes as he struggles to prop himself up. Willow is leaning against the bedroom doorway, her long dark hair down, dressed in an orange slouchy alpaca blend turtleneck, jeans and knee high brown leather boots. She's holding a coffee mug. He looks over at the empty bed across the room. "Where's Zach?"

"He's been up for bit. He just headed down to the restaurant; the guys are keeping him company." Willow says as she appraises his well inked naked body that's exposed above the covers.

Frank rubs his eyes, struggling to clear his vision. "What time is it?"

"Its noon," Willow answers. "You must be starving yourself?"

"What!" Frank says, about to jump out before remembering he has nothing on under the comforter and slouches back down.

Willow laughs. "Relax you don't have to rush off anywhere. I'll give you some privacy. I'll be out in the living room waiting for you. Oh, this coffee's for you. I wasn't sure what you take but Zach said cream and sugar." She sets in on the night stand for him.

"Thanks." Frank says. He can't help but notice how great she smells as she bends down close to set it down. An invisible spark of electricity seems to surge through him with her so near. It's a sensation he hasn't experienced for a long time.

There's a moment of silence as they look at each other. "I'll just wait out here…out there, for you." She smiles pointing out and leaves closing the door behind her.

"Ouch." Frank says, not referring to any pain but the impression she's made on him. It's definitely a good one.

There's a quick rap on the door before Willow pokes her head back in. "The guys left you some clothes on the dresser, not sure what'll fit but gives you something fresh to throw on." She says before ducking back out.

"Thanks again!" He shouts back. He clambers out and empties the coffee mug in two gulps. He tries on the jeans and is surprised after a couple tries that a pair fits. With his meaty round butt and thick muscular thighs he usually finds it difficult to find ones that are comfortable. He brushes his teeth, throws water on his face and looks in the mirror. "Screw it." He says. Ten minutes later he puts on a t-shirt and a lined plaid shirt and emerges from the washroom displaying a clean shaven face revealing his strong jaw line and cleft chin. With his short burr hairstyle, he makes quite a different image and it's difficult for Willow to hide her appreciation for it.

"Wow. You clean up pretty good. You look way younger without the beard. Aren't you concerned about being recognized though?" She asks.

"Yes and no. The teams had my pictures but the Committee can't distribute them to the local authorities, how would they explain me being alive after saying I was dead and they had cornered the terrorist responsible. Plus I didn't hang around places like this so I think the odds are in my favor." He gazes into a mirror in the room. "I haven't seen this face in a while." He says smiling rubbing his jaw with the palm of his hand. "I don't know whose razor I used but I helped myself."

Before he can say anything else, Willow walks past him to the door, giving his butt a pat along the way. "Quit admiring yourself handsome. We better get down stairs. We don't want to give them the wrong idea as to what's taking us so long." She says coyly.

They enter the restaurant and see their group has a back booth by the corner windows. The three don't appear like they were conversing too much. Willow slides in beside Oin and Frank sits beside Zack who's facial stubble is gone too, Stogie Man is on a chair on the end in the aisle.

"I had to look twice who Willow was walking in with." Stogie Man said.

"Yea, time for a change. You're looking leaner, what happened to that gut of yours you were displaying so proudly? Looks like you slimmed down pretty quick." Frank says.

"Things aren't always what they appear." Stogie Man quips.

They're interrupted by the server who comes by, pours them coffee, tops up the others and takes Frank's and Willow's order. The other three are already well into their meals.

"Yea, I am noticing that more and more. So what names are we using for everybody? Still Oin I hope?" Frank asks.

"That's correct." Oin says giving Frank a mock salute.

"And you?" Frank asks referring to Stogie Man.

"How have you been referring to me? I should add; something that can be repeated in public." Stogie Man laughs.

"Actually, I've been calling you Stogie Man because of that stinky cigar you had hanging constantly out of your mouth. Really, how do you do it?" Frank says.

"Again, that one was for appearances." Stogie Man says as he pulls a claro from his shirt pocket. "These are what I normally use." As he hands it to Frank. "They're made from a combination of fruit and vegetable leaves. I gnaw on them because they help me think." Stogie Man chuckles.

Frank takes a whiff of it. The aroma is actually quite pleasant and reminds him of Padoo fruit from the Caribbean, a large pea pod looking fruit that tastes like vanilla. He hands it back.

"Stogie Man huh. I can live with that but let's shorten it to Stogie to keep things simple. I don't want to confuse you too much." Stogie Man says laughing with his barbed words.

"Thanks." Frank replies sarcastically. "So, what's the deal here?" Frank asks. "Who are you all working for? Obviously you have resources and seem to show up whenever to prod me one way or the other. I mean, how did you know I would take the call about the body in the park or know where I was in San Francisco?"

Willow, Oin and Stogie look at one another, stalling the answer they know Zach can provide. Since the time Zach hung with the three of them upstairs while Frank was sleeping and then with the pair down here, he figured out who they were. They weren't blatant about it but they didn't try and hide the subject matter of their conversations either. Zach nudges Frank in the side with his elbow.

"What? I'm trying to get some answers here." Frank says glaring at Zach before directing his attention back to the other three. "What's with the charade? The stoner act in the park, the tourist routine on the highway? Your there when I needed the van, like you're waiting for me, what gives?"

Zach places his arm behind Frank, resting it on the back of the booth bench and leans in close. "They're Handlers Frank."

Frank turns to him. "What?"

"They're Handlers." Zach repeats.

It takes a moment for the words to sink in and when they do, the thoughts and emotions Frank felt when he first learned from the Orb of what they've done to preserve man for the greater good and the millions sacrificed, come flooding back. "You fucking kidding me?" Frank says. He's getting a foul taste in his mouth.

Willow nods her acknowledgement.

He looks around the table. "This is … I need some air … the stench in here is getting too thick." He slides out and heads for the exit.

Willow sighs, "You all wait here." She says as she gets up to follow him.

Zach, Oin and Stogie watch through the windows as Frank stomps past them outside and around the corner to the rear of the lodge in the direction of a storage shed and the garbage containers. Willow is not far behind. Stogie moves in beside Oin so he has a better view.

"This is going to be interesting." Oin says.

Zach is happy sitting tucked away in the corner where he is and has no interest in watching the drama. The problem for Zach is that he feels like an open target staying here so close to Rainier. Sure Frank believes he has little chance of being recognized even though he worked this area for so long but, its Zach the Committee is actively hunting for as its Zach that has all the information on the Committee. It's him that has Mr. H's journals, the research he recovered from the Roswell Revelations, the DNA profile of what the Solomons created in the lab and the match to Frank. In hindsight, it was stupid of him allowing the drone to feed the video back to Belette because now they know he's tied in with the Tsiatko and verified the Orb is in their hands, with him standing right beside it. With Frank standing beside him … they'll probably back track wondering why Zach lied and let him live and whether it was Frank or Zach who killed his associates. They'll question if it just was a coincidence that Frank found the cache and castle, they'll start digging and maybe he'll end up losing whatever advantage he thought he had over them.

His fucking smug attitude is going to come back and bite him in the ass, maybe taking out too big a chunk to recover from. He watches Oin and Stogie being entertained by Willow and Frank. He's not sure what he's up against with these Handlers or what they're capable of but he's positive they'll want the Orb back so if he sticks close to them, it may give him the inside track of recovering it for himself. After all, they're only human and probably can be taken out just like anyone else. This may be his only saving grace from all this… his only out. Whether he can use this as damage control with the Committee and buy his way back in or go solo when he gets the Orb, he'll have to play that by ear. His other edge is that the Handlers don't know what he knows. That could go down the tube if Frank spills everything he knows about him to Willow. He needs to get Frank alone and persuade him to keep his mouth shut.

Willow catches up to Frank and grabs him by the arm, stopping him. There's a heated exchange of words, there's no misinterpreting that.

"Shit!" Stogie says. "We gotta go."

Zach turns to see Frank writhing on the ground with Willow kneeling beside him.

"I can't believe she zapped him." Oin says, throwing a C-note on the table as he gets out.

Zach follows them as they hustle their way to the scene.

"Take him up to the room." Willow instructs them as they arrive.

Oin and Stogie each grab an arm and sling it over their shoulders as they pull Frank upright, balancing his weight between them as they head back to the lodge. Frank is barely conscious, unaware of his surroundings.

"Don't look at me like that." Willow says sharply to Zach. "Just get up to the room and get the door open for them."

Zach does as he's told and scampers ahead of the group, going for the stairs. The rest have no choice but to head through the lobby to access the elevators, the stairs will be too difficult.

"Is everything okay?" One of the front desk staff asks.

"No, all is good." Stogie says as they move past. "Our friend here has low blood sugar, he gets in these moods where he forgets his meds and this is the end result."

"We can call a doctor?" The employee says.

"Not needed, but thanks. We've been through this before. He just needs a chocolate bar or two; some orange juice and a little rest and he'll be good to go." Stogie says.

They wait in awkward silence for the elevator. It arrives and they load Frank, who is starting to become a bit more alert. Zach has the room door open and waiting when they arrive and Willow has them drop Frank on his bed.

"Give us some privacy here." Willow orders. They get out and she closes the bedroom door behind them, leaving them waiting in the living room.

"TV anyone, should be a game on." Oin says crashing on the couch.

"Sure." Stogie replies and takes a seat in the leather chair.

Zach isn't sure what he should do…fuck it. He opens the mini bar, grabs a couple of airplane size bottles of whiskey and takes a spot on the couch as well. He may as well enjoy things while he can.

"Ugh." Frank groans as he struggles to get himself propped up against the head board. His head is a mess and he clearly remembers the last time he felt this way. It was when Zach's men tasered him. Not as extreme this time, but still the same. He looks over at Willow sitting on the edge of the other bed. She has a somber and serious look on her face.

"How are you feeling?" She asks.

"What did you do to me?" Frank says.

Willow extracts her weapon from the back of her waistband, the same one Frank saw at Rainier. "Like I told you, it's a high tech Taser gun. It directs an electrical current through the air like a shock wave specifically targeting the subject. You can set the concentration, no wires like the style they use here and these aren't single shot devices either. They're pretty effective." She says.

"And why the hell did you figure you should do that?" Franks demands.

"Because you were being a dick and talking about leaving, I couldn't have that!" Willow states.

"I had the right to be a dick…because you're Handlers! Christ, all the fucking people you're responsible for killing…what, I should be alright with that?!" Frank says.

As Frank and Willow's exchange echoes into the other room, Oin turns down the TV so they can hear the conversation. He's interested to see how it all goes. Zach is as well.

Willow moves across to his bed. "Open your damn eyes Frank! I hate to burst your bubble but you really aren't part of the population here! You were CREATED to assist in preventing their downfall! You're a tool, a means to the end, a conduit between the Tsiatko and humans! Something your Mr. H had the intuition to carry through with which is why he brought the Solomons on board!" She half yells at him.

Frank is taken aback by her statement. The truth does hurt.

"And you think we enjoy what we do?" Willow continues. "If it wasn't for people like us, ones who VOLUNTEERED for this shit … if we hadn't done what we've done, mankind would have been wiped out thousands of years ago here and untold planets ago."

"But the price for Christ's sake, how do you live with it?" Frank asks.

Willow stands, crossing her arms as she faces Frank, "Live with it?! Are you kidding me?! We, us Handlers, didn't screw up every world these people have lived on … they did. What they are and what we are is night and day. We're stuck doing constant damage control so don't get high and mighty on me. And like us, you're supposed to be part of the solution and that hasn't worked out too well in the past either."

"Are you saying I've been through this before? Tell me … how am I supposed to make a difference because if I did this before, I remember shit, I don't have a fucking clue?" Frank says exasperated.

"You're not supposed to remember, you're not like us and I can't say for sure. It changes every time, more so on this one."

"Seriously?" Frank asks amazed.

Willow sits again. "Look, we're doing things differently this time and not by choice. For the first time we're working without the Orb and this world has technology they not supposed to have yet. The Tsiako are a different version than their ancestors, you're here decades before planned so, it's all screwed up but maybe that's a good thing … maybe that'll make the difference this time."

"Well, that sounds really promising." Frank says, not attempting to hide the sarcasm in his voice.

"Look, like it or not, we need to work together on this. You have to park your pissy greater than thou attitude because we're running out of time. I mean it's not like it's all going to come crashing down tomorrow but sooner than most realize." Willow states.

Frank purposely bangs his head back against the headboard. "What the fuck did I get myself into?" He asks to no one in particular.

"Frank, you had no choice. This was coming your way whether you wanted it or not." Willow replies.

This sucks but it doesn't take a lot of reflection for him to realize the woman is right about it all. He preferred judging when he was on the outside looking in but now, he's right in the thick of things. "And you really believe we're…they're worth it?" Frank asks reminding himself that he's not really part of the civilization here. "That going through all this…time and time again merits it?"

Willow hesitates before answering. "I have asked myself that question so many times…and I've always come up with the same answer. Yes."

"And what happens if you, if we, actually succeed this time?" Frank asks.

"You lost me. What do you mean?"

"What happens to you?"

"Hopefully," Willow says smiling, "I get to reclaim my life, to just live and then…I get to die."

CHAPTER TWENTY-ONE

"Ms. Byrnes?" Bertram's voice comes through over the speaker phone.

"Yes?"

"As you requested, Mr. Scott is here to see you."

"Thank you. Send him in."

There's a rap on the door, "Ma'am." Garth says as he enters.

"Come in and have a seat." Reggie says. She's just finishing off a tapioca pudding and tosses the empty container as Scott takes a chair at her desk. "Eating on the run." She says, finishing things off with a drink of lemon water.

"I can imagine as you've been quite busy." Scott says.

"Yes." Reggie says with a smile. "All good things though."

Scott just nods. It's no secret how Felix Belette went down.

"Just to clear the air, you have any problems with being shuffled around?"

"Of course not, you know me." Scott emphasizes.

"You have anyone on payroll that can assume your current position?"

Scott thinks for a moment. "Yea, there is."

"Good. I need you to put a team together for me. Twenty individuals that won't mind getting their hands dirty. I need a group to do fieldwork. You'll be heading it. Pull from where you need, hire if you have to and I'm sure I don't have to remind you that they must be thoroughly vetted if you do. But, I guess I just did, didn't I?" Reggie says.

"I understand." Garth replies.

"I knew you would. And it should go without saying but I'll say it anyways, don't compromise the security here doing this."

"Have some faith in me. How soon do you need the team?" Scott asks.

"Urgently."

"Anything else?"

"No, that should do it for now."

"I'll get at it then." Scott says getting up.

"Just don't let anything fall through the cracks, okay? It's important." Reggie adds sincerely.

"Have I ever?" Scott says reassuringly.

Reggie smiles as Scott closes the door behind him.

Before 9/11 the Committee pulled resources from any agency they chose because their people are embedded in senior positions in every central one in the world. They could because, before 9/11, no agency wanted to share information, everything was kept close to the chest for fear someone else would take the credit for any successes. It was so easy to pull the wool over their eyes. Now, it's all different. Everyone shares everything for fear of missing something and being held to blame, covering their asses. Things change and methods have to change along with them. That's what Felix didn't understand. The old school ways had to go and if you didn't? Well … just ask Felix. That's why Reggie needed a fresh team. She couldn't pull from elsewhere because someone may ask the wrong or right question. The Committee is as powerful an entity as it is for two reasons. One, because of its high ranking personnel that has successfully infiltrated every key law enforcement agency, every major corporation in the world, every branch of the U.S. military and in the governments of most developed countries. Two, they're as dominant of a force as they are because of their veil of secrecy. They're very selective of whom they choose and rarely do their members betray them. And there is another side to those that work for them, ones like Angela Sheppard, the DNA Specialist who only know they work for a powerful unnamed corporation, one that has a zero tolerance policy and they know nothing of the Committee itself. Allmass was unique mix of senior member, independent contractor and worker and now, an unexpected turncoat who knows way more than he should have been allowed to, another reason for Felix's demise. Reggie's job is not about preventing a potential alliance of the Tsiatko with Allmass or Smirnov, whoever or whatever he may turn out to be. The Committee doesn't believe they alone are capable of stopping their Mars exploration programs, the search for other exoplanets, the testing of habitable settlements at NASA, destroying the seed facility or the host of other programs well under way for their relocation. Not that the Committee really wants to test that theory. Her role, in their eyes, is about containment, the restriction of information, maintaining the veil of secrecy that shrouds the Committee and most importantly its plans. And if there is a revolt by the combined forces of the Tsiatko with Allmass's and Smirnov's assistance and possibly other anomalies, her task is to ensure nothing is exposed, primarily the reasons for the revolt. She has to prevent the release of information the Orb may contain and what the revelations of Beings like the Tsiatko could convey to the world besides their very existence. Sure all that would shake the very foundation of man but the Committee is beyond caring about that. It's about them and their members escaping unscathed from this planet's certain death. Its one thing to battle a small revolt but to fight off billions of people is a war that the Committee won't win and that would ultimately result in their relocation plans being doomed. For her, to contain the information is to contain the key players, Allmass and possibly Smirnov. What changes everything now is the appearance of the Handlers. This is a completely different ballgame now and she has no intentions of sharing with the Committee that Allmass and the Tsiatko have more than Smirnov to swing things in their favor. Reggie checks the clock before picking up her cell and calling Angela Sheppard. Her time is up for providing the DNA profile from Smirnov's place.

"Hello?" Ms. Sheppard answers. Her voice sounds…timid, worried even with that single word.

"This is Reggie Byrnes, what do you have for me?"

"Oh…Ms. Byrnes. Uh, not to question your motives but…was this some kind of test to verify my capabilities? I am quite good at my job you know, one of the best in the private sector."

"Excuse me?" Reggie asks.

"I'm sorry. It's just…these results make absolutely no sense and so I have to ask."

"Hang on a minute." Reggie says as she places the cell against her chest and gives herself a moment to think things through. "Angela, I appreciate your patience. Listen, in about an hour and a half, a helicopter will be on the roof pad of your facility to pick you up. A Mr. Scott will be on board to escort you back here."

"Ma'am?" Angela asks.

"Angela, I can't explain this over the phone. It's too sensitive a matter. Make sure you don't discuss your trip with anyone, be on the roof waiting and bring everything with you. All remaining samples, anything and everything related to this. To you understand?"

"Tonight?"

"Yes, tonight. Is that a problem?" Reggie asks sternly.

"No ma'am…uh, it's just…"

"Just what? I don't want to repeat myself. And I mean everything. Wipe any data from your computer and from any others systems and equipment in your lab that were used, am I clear on this?" Reggie says.

"Yes ma'am."

"See you soon." She ends the call and buzzes Bertram.

"Yes?"

"I need Scott back in here right away."

"Consider it done."

Five minutes later, Scott knocks and enters. "You needed me?"

"Your field work is starting now. Take a chopper and pick up an Angela Sheppard from our lab facilities, Bertram will give you the location. She'll be waiting on the roof. Verify she has all the samples, raw and finished, analysis, everything related to the testing I was having her complete with her. She's coming solo and I told her not to discuss it with anyone. Verify that as well." Reggie says.

"And if there's any issues?" Scott asks.

"Take care of them, quietly."

Yes ma'am."

"See you in about…three and half hours." Reggie says checking the time on her cell.

Scott nods and leaves.

Reggie grabs a banana off the table, she needs a proper meal but she's tired. She walks to the office door, opens it and calls out to Bertram at his desk. "I'm having a nap, let me know when Scott and Sheppard are here." She lies on the leather tufted couch nearby where she already has a pillow and a light blanket she's been using. She's dying for some new furnishings, soon she reminds herself, soon. She kicks off her shoes, finishes the banana and drops the peel on the floor. A couple minutes later she's out.

"Ms. Byrnes? Ms. Byrnes?" Bertram repeats himself as he gently shakes her.

Reggie doesn't move, just opens her eyes to see Bertram peering down at her.

"Ms. Byrnes, they're back."

Reggie's head is still partially in slumber land as she lies there unresponsive but with eyes wide open.

"Ms. Byrnes? Mr. Scott and Ms. Sheppard are here."

"How long have I been sleeping? She asks.

"The entire time." Bertram says.

Reggie breaths in deeply. "Ok, give me a few minutes to freshen up."

"Of course." Bertram replies.

Reggie checks the time before heading to the private adjoining washroom. She reemerges feeling better, takes her place at the desk and calls Bertram. "Have Sheppard come in and ask Scott to wait outside."

A moment later, a knock on the door is followed by Bertram letting Angela Sheppard in. Angela is a diminutive individual with short dark hair and big rimmed glasses. She has a nerdy mousy look to her which is a compliment in today's world of technology. She's still wearing her lab coat, her I.D. still hangs from a lanyard around her neck and she has a file folder clutched tightly against her chest. She seems hesitant to approach.

Reggie doesn't bother to stand. "Angela, nothing to fear here. Please have a seat." As she gestures to the chairs in front of her desk.

Angela approaches cautiously. "Sorry, this has all shaken me a bit. This clandestine meeting, the helicopter ride... it's been a bit unnerving."

"I can understand. Sorry for the drama but I assure you, it's necessary."

Angela takes a seat, places the folder on the desk, takes a moment to push up her glasses and runs her fingers through her hair. She's so petite she looks like a child sitting there. Reggie reaches for the file, opens it and flips through until she locates the DNA profile.

"So explain to me what we have here?"

Angela begins to tremble.

"What's the matter?" Reggie asks. "You're obviously scared. Were you threatened in any way?" Hoping Scott was not aggressive with her.

"I'm sorry Ms. Byrnes." Angela says rubbing her temples with her hands, "It's just that..." She takes a deep breath.

"What?" Reggie asks, clearly confused by her reaction.

"Well, I know we aren't suppose to discuss our work not even internally unless it's absolutely required but… I'm sorry, for acting like this but," She takes another deep breath. "A while back another person from the company had a colleague of mine do an analysis that she wasn't suppose to talk about." Angela takes off her glasses to wipe tears from her eyes. "But she told me about it… not the details, just how weird the DNA profile results were… like this one." Angela looks up briefly at Reggie holding back a sob. "She was instructed to bring all the results to him, just like you asked me on this… and then she never came back, she was killed in a carjacking that same night."

Reggie sits back in her chair, taken aback by this revelation."Did she say who it was?"

There is a look of fear on Angela's face. "A man named Allamer? Allamiss? Something along those lines." She sputters out.

Reggie leans forward. "Allmass? Could the name have been Allmass?"

Angela looks surprised. "Yes… that was it. Allmass. Do you know him?"

"Unfortunately yes. He's the reason you're here, you could say. I shouldn't disclose this but I will just to ease your mind a bit. He used to work for us but went astray, killed a number of people and was possibly hiding out at the residence I had you pull samples from. We're not sure what game he's playing but we suspect he's been using messed up DNA to throw us off the scent but in turn, we've been using that as a means to trail him." Reggie lies.

"Oh my God." Angela exclaims as she exhales deeply. "I feel so much better." She smiles waving her hand across her face to cool down her flushed feeling. "You know I… I actually thought… something was going to happen to me. I was so scared but I didn't know what to do."

"Well, I'm relieved you aren't anymore. So please, explain this profile to me."

"I'll try but there's not much to explain because… I can't really. Fifty-six percent is normal Homo sapiens with a wide mix of ethnic origins which can be typical but almost twenty percent is Neanderthal which is unheard of or even possible as far as I know. Most of us have some form of Neanderthal DNA due to our ancestral roots, the average is two percent. On extremely rare occasions five percent has been found… but twenty? I can't even imagine." Angela explains.

"And the remaining?" Reggie asks.

"The last twenty-five is unknown."

"What do you mean unknown?"

"That's the only way I can describe it, unknown. I mean there is an even rarer strain of DNA that is suspected to be a cousin of the Neanderthal called the Denisovans and there has been DNA recovered from a finger bone and a few teeth in Siberia and matches made but only to people in Melanesia near Asia and again, three percent tops. This doesn't match that though."

"So what do you suspect this last percentile is?" Reggie says.

"My best guess is some kind of an extinct species of humanoid and I only say this because it's branched with other human DNA. I mean twenty percent Neanderthal is impossible enough because to recover this sample would mean something recent… Neanderthals have been extinct for forty-thousand years. I don't even know how someone could fake that aspect of the profile and I can't even fathom anything plausible to explain the twenty-five percent unknown."

"I can… it's the final piece to the puzzle." Reggie murmurs to herself.

"What was that ma'am?" Angela asks.

"Oh, sorry, I was thinking to myself. You're right, how's it possible? This does help though."

"I'm so relieved I could assist. I tell you, this really had me worked up." Angela says placing her hands on her chest.

Reggie dials Bertram. "Can you come get Ms. Sheppard and have her wait while I discuss matters with Mr. Scott before they leave?"

Bertram and Scott enter and Bertram takes Angela outside, closing the door behind them. Scott takes a seat at the desk.

Reggie extracts a page from the file and hands it to Scott. "Sheppard is wearing her lab I.D., make sure you get her password then go through the lab tonight and make sure that file is nowhere to be found."

"This 37A42X?" Scott asks referring to the paper.

"Yes."

"I'll dispose of her before I do that. I don't need the extra baggage while I'm getting it done… too much could go wrong." Scott says.

Reggie fixes her gaze on Scott, "I don't want her body found, ever." She stipulates.

CHAPTER TWENTY-TWO

Frank slides over to the side of the bed and sits up facing Willow. He rubs his hands over his face and head. "I hate being tasered." He knows as much as he has mix feelings about what the Handlers have done, he realizes it is the bigger picture that matters and he has a critical role in it whether he likes it or not. He has to accept he can't let it get personal regardless how tough the task or what decisions he'll have to make along the way.

Willow reaches across and puts a hand on his lap. "Will it help if I say I'm… sort of sorry for stunning you?" She says half convincingly.

"No… but I'll get payback one day," He replies. "Handlers huh, so where's your spaceship?

"If I told you, I'd have to kill you." She says smirking.

"So… what now?" Frank asks.

"How about we eat, I'm starving."

"Deal, just please, no more with that gun of yours if I'm not cooperating."

"Agreed, I'll use a bat." Willow winks as she leads the way out of the bedroom.

"What's the verdict?" Stogie asks as they come out.

"He's on board, with some convincing." Willow says smiling. "We keep pushing ahead.

"Frank, you got a minute?" Zach asks trying to get a word in with him before he talks too much with Willow.

"Has to wait. We're going down to eat." Frank says.

"Two minutes Frank, just two minutes." Zach replies.

"Zach… whatever it is, it can wait." Frank answers.

"How about some company then?" Zach asks hoping he can at least eliminate any talk that may concern him.

"Uh, no." Frank responds. "We need some privacy." As he leads Willow by the arm to the door.

"I'm out of here too." Stogie says. "I'll be in my room if you need me."

"Me as well." Oin says and they leave Zach to himself. Once they're out in the hallway "Is it safe leaving him alone?" Oin whispers.

"Yea," Frank says. "He's got nowhere to go."

Willow and Frank make their way downstairs leaving Oin and Stogie in the hallway. "Do you trust him?" Willow asks.

"Not really."

"Then why partner up with him?"

"I guess…because, I had no other choice."

Over food, Frank reveals to Willow the entire Rainier story including Mr. H's journals, how he ended up with Zach and they're escape from the Tsiatko. He tells her everything he knows about Zach but doesn't go into his life before Rainier or his childhood even though he suspects she knows most everything about him and these events already. He's not sure why. He knows the Handlers priority is the big picture, mankind as a whole and he has seen the evidence that anyone can be the sacrificial lamb to them and in the end, possibly even him but as much as he prods; she won't divulge much about his role. She doesn't want him to have any preconceived notions about anything, that Fate can still play a part. He finds it strange that even with an advanced civilization, one that the Handlers were created from, Fate is still considered a critical factor or that they'd have such strong beliefs in something so…veiled, elusive and mystical. Frank is getting frustrated though. He wants some real answers. "You must be able to tell me something, Christ, anything. The Orb, what about that then? Why haven't the Tsiatko done anything with it? Or, now that you know where it is, why aren't you trying to recover it?"

"Because we've decided we shouldn't have it back. We're doing things differently than we have before. It's where it needs to be, for now." Willow replies.

"For fuck sakes." Frank says exasperated. "Enough with the half answers already; give me something, anything I can use and let me figure it out from there then."

Willow reluctantly nods okay. "Walk with me." She says. As they go through the lobby, she spots Oin and Stogie tucked away in a corner spying on them, Frank doesn't. She motions for them to quit as they make their way out to the SUV. They climb in and she fires it up so they have some warmth. She blows into her cupped hands waiting for the truck to heat up. "No one to hear us here."

Oin and Stogie watch from the lobby. "Are they going somewhere?" Oin asks.

"Don't have a clue… don't have a clue." Stogie mutters.

"What do you think they're discussing?" Oin asks.

Stogie removes the unlit cigar and gives him a look. "How the hell would I know? You want to go out there and ask? Maybe, they just want some privacy."

Zach watches from his room as Frank and Willow walk to the SUV. He's wondering similar things. "What are they talking about and how much has Frank told her?"

"The Orb is the last resort for the Tsiatko. "Willow says. "Unlike their ancestors, they don't have the capability of leaving this planet. That's why they haven't done anything with it."

"You're losing me again. What do you mean by last resort?"

"If they touch the Orb, the planet and everything on it is gone. It's like a safety net. They're not permitted to access its contents. We do… did consider them the enemy. They touch it, it goes into self destruct.

"You mean like a nuclear device?"

"Way more than that. A planet killer. Everything goes. There's no protection from it. No bunker of any type can protect anyone or anything." Willow says.

"Son of a bitch… so that's why Brother refused. So explain to me… WHY are you leaving it with them?"

"It has been taken from us before due to circumstances beyond our control during other occupations and when we had attempted to recover it, we were unsuccessful and all was lost. So we decided we're leaving it where it is. The Tsiatko have had it for quite some time, as you have said. They've done nothing more than protect it, waiting for you I imagine. You said yourself, they value all life. It's only humans they despise for what they have done to this world. They're not prepared to commit suicide or wipe out all other life… not yet anyways."

"Why wait for me?"

"Because you're the balance. You're here to enlighten them, to enlighten the world. You're a combination of old and new, the past and the present, human and Tsiatko and everything in between. You alone can access ALL the Orb contains without activating the destruction mode unless you will it. You have the choice, they do not and we do not.

"What do you mean will it?" Frank asks as he turns toward her.

"Mentally will it but you have to be in physical contact with it at the same time. You'll see in time, the more you use the Orb, the more it syncs with you. It's designed to interface with you specifically."

"What do you mean I will see in time?"

"Shit, I'm getting ahead of myself." She answers. "At some point and time, if all goes well, you will have the opportunity to learn what all it contains and it's more than you can imagine."

"When, how?" Frank asks.

Willow is showing her frustration now. "I can't tell you because I don't know for sure! Everything has to find its natural course as oxymoron as that statement is!"

"Fine, we'll just leave it at that then. Can it be deactivated or defused?"

"No. Any attempt to destroy it, no matter how ingenious a method someone believes they have devised will only put it into destruction mode…and it can't be defused."

"And why exactly did you think you needed to create such a thing and why someone like me as the potential trigger man?"

"A control mechanism. A means to reset the entire process with someone who can be regarded as neutral who is neither of this world or the Tsiatko's but something in the middle that can give everything consideration. Maybe not the most prudent but the most logical considering the circumstances. The destruction is not immediate. It takes five years for the full detonation as it goes through a multitude of impact stages."

"Five years, why so long and how do you know it already isn't set?" Frank asks.

"The colour. You said it's blue, that's the safe mode yet. Believe it or not, some colours are universal regardless of the civilization. If it was activated, it would be emitting an amber glow that would eventually change to a bright red hue."

"You're not doing anything to lighten the situation with all this." Shaking his head as he sits back in the seat.

Willow continues. "Five years may seem like a long time to you but not to us Handlers or the Tsiatko. Five years is like a week to the Tsiatko compared to your life span, not much different to us Handlers considering how long we've been around and how much would have to be accomplished to prepare in such a short time."

"So I have set it off every other time before?"

"No, you never have. It was the Tsiatko's forefathers who did by sacrificing one of their own to do the task, before they made their escape from those other planets even though you were there in one form or another. They did it in hopes of ridding themselves of humans but it didn't work because we Handlers were there to ensure things carried on. We didn't realize it at first but we were following them because we were simply moving to the nearest most habitable planet, the same as they were."

"Who or what were they?" Franks asks.

"We didn't encounter them until the last … half dozen occupations. They're not many in number and they highly appreciated life but then again, any species can only take so much. We never put a name to them but they were a force to be reckoned with. It was only our technology that kept them at bay and ultimately was used against us."

"What happened before them?" Frank says.

"Before them doesn't matter." Willow replies flatly.

"Okay, excuse me for asking. So what happened to them here?"

"We don't know. We believe they may have purposely mated with the Neanderthal to create the Tsiatko and then those that were left, left, forcing their prodigy to work it out if a new population arrived here. Maybe they were sick of it all too, the constant running, tired of moving, tired of fighting, hoping something would change, something for the better." Willow says. "Maybe they're forcing everyone to make their last stand on this world. There's no hint as to where they may have gone to, maybe they just wanted to live out their existence in peace."

"You have to get the Orb off this planet." Frank demands.

Willow smiles, "Sorry Frank, not your call. It stays. This WILL be the last stand. Either mankind makes it here or perishes here. Well, that's if we can stop the Committee."

"So what do I do?"

"You'll do what you need to do when the time is right."

"Fuck! I've heard the same similar shit from Brother and now you!" Frank shouts as he starts punching the dashboard. "Not a damn clear answer anywhere."

"Frank, stop, you can't be pounding the dash like that." She says, reaching out to gently grab is arm and momentarily halting his physical destruction. "Based on what you told me, Brother seems like a wise…individual. We both see something in you that you haven't realized yet so just accept it."

"What, you're worried about your rental insurance! I'll vent as I please!" As he gives the dashboard once final blow, activating the passenger air bag which propels him back hard against the seat and covers him in a fine white mist.

Willow shuts off the truck, jumps out coughing waving her hand to clear the haze that is following her and hits the fob to stop the alarm that was automatically activated. "That's why! She yells at him. "I warned you!"

Frank is pushing and punching on the bag in exasperation so he can access the door and get out himself. He finally succeeds, exiting coated in the white powder, slamming the door shut behind him. Zach, Oin and Stogie watch in amazement from their perches, not sure if they should even attempt to assist. Frank stares at her across the hood. It's the first time she's seen his eyes jet black and it shakes her up a bit. It reminds her that she's dealing with someone beyond human. He stomps off to his room to hose off and Willow proceeds to the lobby where Oin and Stogie still wait.

"Not sure that went well, whatever it was you were trying to do." Stogie says. "You okay?"

"I'm fine." Willow says. "I can't imagine learning all he's learnt in such a short time. He's actually taking it pretty good." She giggles thinking about how Frank looked after the air bag exploded. "I need to go clean up." As she brushes some of the powder off her clothing. "Here," she tosses them the fob. "We're going to need a replacement ride."

Frank bursts into his room to a waiting Zach. Zach sees Frank's black orbs. "Don't say a fucking word!" Frank says pointing a finger in Zach's direction as he storms past him. "Not a fucking word!" Frank stops a few steps past Zach, wheels around and grabs him by the throat, shoving him against the wall."Did you know it ACTUALLY has the potential of being a bomb?!" Frank demands.

Zach is struggling to breath, never mind speak and it takes both hands to push against Frank's one to give him some air. "Know what was a bomb?" He rasps out.

Frank presses hard. "The Orb, the fucking Orb…did you and the Committee know, it's a goddamn world killing, fucking…wipe out everything explosive device?" He rasps out.

Zach hits Frank's arm down hard in order to break free. "What the hell's the matter with you?" As he massages his throat. "No, I had no idea. You think I would've touched it if I did…is that what Willow said?"

Frank points his finger in Zach's face. The veins on his throat are enlarged, his eyes still black and his face flushed red, still coated in white along with his hair every other part of him. "Fuck!" He says before heading to the bathroom, slamming the door behind him.

"I've had enough." Zach says checking to ensure his automatic is still safely secured as he heads to Willow's room. "It's time for my own questions." He knocks hard on her door while the other hand firmly grasps the butt of the gun in his back waistband.

Willow opens the door and immediately places her weapon tight under his chin. "Ease your hand off that gun…or not, I'd love to fry your brains out Zach." She warns.

He does as he's told.

Willow makes a quick inspection of his neck. "Frank's been a little rough on you and now you've come to take it out on me. I can hear…I'm just next door, remember?"

Before he realizes it, Stogie and Oin are on either side of him and have a solid hold on his arms. They were on their way up, hauling the weapons from the back of the SUV in reinforced garbage bags. They steer him inside and Stogie stays behind him as Oin goes to retrieve their cargo. Willow hasn't let up the pressure of her weapon under his chin.

"What were you going to do Zach?" Willow whispers loudly in his ear as Stogie extracts Zach's weapon.

"Answers, I just wanted some answers, I'm tired of sitting in the dark." He replies.

"Oh Zach…your far from sitting in the dark. I suspect you're playing everyone aren't you?" Willow says.

Zach says nothing, only stares back at her. Zach wonders what she knows. Willow isn't giving him any hints.

"Frank is an important individual, but you already know that. Make sure you don't do anything to jeopardize that but…you know that already too. If its survival you're worried about, you're going to have to pick a side pretty soon…but you may already realize that as well. I'm sure you're weighing all your options. Things are coming to a head soon Zach and you're better start deciding where you should hedge your bets…with us, with them…on your own, decisions, decisions, decisions." Willow says.

Zach knows it's another one of those times for him to just shut up.

"You may think we're just human but I'd advise you to think again before you act." She says as she lowers her weapon. "Give him back his gun."

Stogie gives her a questioned look. "I'd love for him to try." She says over Zach's shoulder to him.

Zach turns as Stogie reluctantly does and he quickly exits making his way away to the stairs.

"Was that wise?" Oin asks.

"Yes." Willow says. "I have plans for him now and he may be of some use after all. We'll need transportation."

"We're on it." Stogie says and they leave.

"Could I have done anything more stupid?" Zach says to himself as he goes down to the lounge. It's time to find a dark corner, have a drink and lick his wounds. He has no other escape right now.

A half hour later Willow knocks on the adjoining door to Frank's room. She figures he's had enough time to cool off. "Frank? Let me in. I could be rude and just walk in the front door, it is registered to me." A minute later a shirtless Frank opens the door. "Okay. I'm good with this look too." She comments before brushing past him, taking a seat on the couch, her weapon draped over her lap. "I won't need this will I?" She asks.

Frank throws a shirt on. "Funny…what now, more riddles and games?" He asks, still frustrated but knowing things have to move forward.

"Sorry. Trying to lighten the mood." As she places it on the coffee table. "Do you trust us Frank? Trust me?"

Frank leans back on a cabinet and takes a moment to rub his chin before answering. "No offense but I don't trust anyone, old habits."

"Oh. Not the answer I was expecting."

Frank gives a small smile. "My poor attempt at lightening the mood." He lies.

Willow smiles back. "I guess we both suck at humor."

"Do I really trust you? I do, sort of." Frank lies again. "I don't know. Do I have a lot of choice right now? Part of me wants to punch every wall in this place, toss some furniture around, inflict some damage…beat the crap out of somebody." He rubs his brows with his fingers, trying to massage out some of the stress. "Find a puppy to kick." He jokes.

"How about this instead? Are you game for testing the waters of Fate and try and do some damage to the Committee at the same time?" She asks.

"What do you have in mind?"

She tells Frank of her recent encounter with Zach.

"Are you alright?" He asks.

"What? Tell me you didn't ask me that because I'm a woman?"

"Sorry, sorry." He answers holding his arms up in defense.

"There's only one out of the five of us that isn't as critical to the big picture…not so far anyways. So why don't we use him as bait and a little payback at the same time. See where it goes?"

"And what would that involve?"

"Let's return him back to the where he once came, send him back to the wolves." Willow says.

"Care to expand?"

She does.

"I like…and I have just the thing in my medical kit that'll help." Frank says.

CHAPTER TWENTY-THREE

"What to do, what to do, what to do?" Reggie thinks tapping a pencil on the desk. She's back in her soon to be revamped office. It's a new day and she's feeling refreshed after a solid sleep. She's still undecided whether to keep it her bedroom or take over and redo Felix's. Her current thoughts are about Allmass and Smirnov, not about her room and decorating options. She has her heels up on the desk as she takes a sip of coffee, which has the perfect blend of cream and cane sugar, allowing the caffeine to get her mind stimulated. It's amazing how that seems to work at the start of the day; it's hard for her to function without it. She follows it with a bite from an oatmeal cereal bar which seems extremely tasty as well. Everything is pretty good so far and she wonders if it's a sign of things to come. Well, she knows Allmass is with Smirnov more than just because he's a childhood friend and a deadly hit man. Smirnov is some kind of lab creation, a mix of Neanderthal, human and obviously Tsiatko. That would explain how they were able to team up with those creatures even with Allmass's history with them. She has to believe Smirnov potentially has other talents as well that have contributed to his reputation as a hired gun. And now a team of Handlers are involved with them. She's sure Allmass is of little interest to them, he's just caught up in the mix. Reggie smiles, this may get interesting; she thought all the Handlers had abandoned this project decades ago. I guess some don't like to give up or be sent off with their tails between their legs. Maybe there's something to be said about pride in one's work and seeing things through to the end. She understands that. And the Tsiatko have the Orb, it was sitting there in plain sight in the video. She wonders why the Handler's haven't recovered it yet…leaving well enough alone maybe. So where is everybody? Where could they be? Of course there are

Tsiatko still in Rainier but what is the rest of this oddball group up to? She needs something to bait a trap and see what gets snared. Bertram buzzes her and she swings down her feet to pick up the call. "Yes?"

"Ms. Byrnes, Sherriff Barton, from Ashford is on the phone. He's says it's urgent he talks to you directly. I tried to say you were detained but he demands I interrupt you."

"Really? Put him through and we'll see what the mighty Sherriff finds so important." Reggie says as she takes the call. "Morning Sherriff, I'm surprised getting this call so early in the day. How are matters in Ashford?" She adds more to amuse herself as opposed to any real curiosity.

"Well Ms. Byrnes…thanks for asking. To be honest, I'm surprised by your interest."

"Sherriff, I may come off as harsh but it's the job, you understand. The pressures that go with a senior position, as you well know I'm sure." She says smiling. Oh, the delight she takes in playing people.

"I do, I do. That's why I needed to contact you immediately and directly. Uh, we have your Agent Allmass in our cells. I'm not sure if you knew he was missing."

"Pardon me?" Reggie exclaims.

"We…have your NSA Agent Zachariah Allmass?" The Sherriff repeats hesitantly.

"Are you sure?"

"Absolutely. I spent some time with him in person when he was down interviewing our missing deputy. Allmass said I was of great assistance." Barton boasts.

"How, why?" Reggie asks in amazement.

'Well ma'am, not much to it really. We received a call that a person was sleeping on a bench in the town square this morning. It's still quite cold out and there were concerns about it possibly being a body. I was driving into work as the medics were there so I stopped. I recognized Allmass immediately. He was wrapped in a blanket, still warm. He couldn't have been there long, minutes even."

"So to confirm. He's alive?"

"Very much so but it appears he's been heavily sedated. There's some recent bruising on his neck and an obvious needle puncture mark as well."

"How long ago was this?"

"Half hour maybe."

"And why do you have him in your cells?" Reggie asks.

"Well, I was going to have him transported to the hospital but since the medics confirmed he was not in any medical distress, just drugged and because of everything that's been going on around here lately, I thought it would be safer to keep him here for his own protection."

Reggie sits back in her chair a bit dumbfounded. "Sherriff, I hope you like bourbon because I'm sending you a bottle of the best."

"Oh, why thank you ma'am … matter of fact I do."

"Sherriff don't let anyone near him or let him out. You understand?"

"No worries plus the medics said whatever's in his system, he'll be down for awhile, he's out cold."

"Really? Do you have the resources to do a drug screening for what he may have been injected with?"

"We sure do." Barton answers proudly.

"Can it be put on top of the list so we can get some results ASAP?"

"Absolutely."

"Thanks Sherriff. I am sending a team by helicopter, headed by a man named Garth Scott. They should be there in a couple hours or so to transport Allmass back to us. Keep him safe for me."

"Anything for you ma'am, anything for you."

"Sherriff, talk to you soon." Reggie lies hanging up.

Reggie calls Bertram's extension. "I need Scott in here right away and dig up the best bottle of bourbon you can find in this place. Belette liked his booze and only the best. He must have a stash somewhere."

"Pardon?" Bertram replies.

"You heard me. Scott and bourbon." She hangs up and giggles, suddenly realizing that may have come out wrong.

Minutes later Garth Scott knocks and enters. He's carrying a bottle of Booker's Bourbon. "Bertram handed me this, I didn't ask why."

"It's for the Sherriff in Ashford. I need you to take a chopper and get down there right away. He has Allmass in his cells."

"How?" Scott asks.

"Found him drugged on a bench. It's a set up of some type so watch your back. Don't be shy on who and what you have to take. Just get him back here."

"Consider it done." Scott says leaving.

"What are they up to?" She's wonders. "And why are they throwing Allmass back…alive?"

Frank, Willow, Stogie and Oin are parked a block down from the Sherriff's office in Ashford. They have a clear enough view of its front between the trees that are partially concealing them. They're in a full size late model tan Dodge Caravan with tinted windows that Oin and Stogie traded out in Seattle. It blends in pretty well. They had followed the ambulance here from where they'd left Zach in the town square. The third row seating feature in this model came in pretty handy. It wasn't difficult to convince Zach to join them to do some recon regardless of the previous day's events. He was in the middle row with Frank and Willow in the back. They let him get comfortable and feeling relaxed as they cruised and Willow simply grabbed his forehead from behind and emptied the syringe into his neck. Good old Midazolam, a very strong sedative that Frank had in his medical kit along with a wide range of other potential medical needs. He's used it before on some of his victims. Zach will be out for a good five to six hours and a nice side affect is its severe amnesic properties. Zach won't remember much about what happened.

Willow followed the injection with popping a high tech microchip down his throat, from the inventory of gadgets the Handlers have. It uses a combination of GPS and radio tracking and will stay in his system for seventy-two hours. It's more advanced then what's available today so it may go undetected by the Committee but that'll remain to be seen. They'll be suspicious as to why Zach has been dropped back in their laps but they're hoping it will lead them to a Committee stronghold.

"We've got movement." Stogie says.

Stogie and Willow are now in front with Frank and Oin behind, concealed by the tinted side windows. A group of vested Deputies exits armed with automatic rifles and lines up down either side of the front entrance as the Sherriff holds the main door open, waiting. Moments later a Bell Helicopter lands out front and a crew decked out the same style vests and automatics, disembark rushing into the office as the deputies remain outside standing guard. Willow, who is watching through binoculars, suddenly lurches forward.

"What?" Stogie asks.

She drops the binoculars momentarily, "Nothing." she says.

Thirty seconds later, the crew re-emerges from the office, dragging a still unconscious Zach among them as they quickly load and depart. Willow is watching intently. She lowers the binoculars, still staring ahead, biting down on her bottom lip.

"What is it?" Stogie asks again. He doesn't have a clear view of things without binoculars.

It takes a moment for Stogie's question to register but she doesn't answer him. "Recognize anyone from the chopper?" Willow asks back to Frank who has binoculars too.

Frank lowers his. "No, they're facing us but moving too fast. One odd looking guy, but I never had much exposure to anyone other than the surveillance I did on Zach in San Francisco."

"It was a long shot, not that it matters." Willow says. She's still staring off in space, her brow furrowed, still chewing on her bottom lip in thought.

"Willow, what?" Stogie asks once more.

She turns to look at Frank before answering Stogie. "Nothing, really. It's just that … we've lived so many lives and I thought … I had recognized someone from the past." She gives her head a slight nod to the side. "I know it was my imagination, still, I had to do a bit of brain searching." She says reassuringly.

"You sure?" Stogie asks.

"Yea, I'm sure." She replies.

"Road trip?" Oin asks excitedly interrupting.

"Road trip." Willow confirms. "Time to pack and check out."

A couple hours later, Reggie watches from her office window as the Bell lands. "Ms. Byrnes." Bertram interrupts, "I just forwarded you the email with the drug screening results on Allmass that the Sherriff sent."

She looks back at him standing in the open office door. "Okay. Tell Scott to bring Allmass in here. I need to have a few words with him before we do anything else." She takes a seat and views the results. "Midazolam … cagey, very smart." She whispers.

Shortly, Scott enters the room with two of the crew hauling Allmass and he instructs them to drop him on the couch. "Guard the door." He tells them closing it behind them and waits inside for Reggie's instructions.

"Well?" Reggie asks from her desk.

"He's starting to come around but just barely."

"No surprise. They used Midazolam on him." Reggie says.

Scott nods his understanding. "What do you want to do?"

Reggie gets up, moves toward Allmass and stops over the figure slumped on the leather sofa, crossing her arms across her chest. Scott notices she makes an impressive looking executive in her black heels, wearing a slim cut turquoise skirt suit, black shirt and layered pearl necklace with her long red hair flowing down on her shoulders. One wouldn't realize how ruthless and deadly a person she actually is. She bends down low to Allmass, gently moving his head back and forth, checking the bruising on his neck and examining the injection site. Once done, she slaps him hard across the face and he moans in response "Zach…you've been a very bad boy." She says, not caring whether he felt the blow or heard her words. She places her hands on her hips looking at Scott. "We'll wait a bit." And takes a seat in the nearby Regency lazy chair and tries to get comfortable. "God," She says to no one in particular, "I need to get this place redone already. How can anyone sit in this thing?"

Scott walks to her desk and pulls an office chair over so he can have a seat near Allmass as well. The two of them sit in silence and wait for Allmass to become more coherent.

"Have we scanned him yet?" Reggie asks.

"Not yet." Scott answers, getting up and opening the office door. "Bring me a hand held scanner." He orders one of the guards before returning to his seat.

Five minutes later there's a knock, the door opens and a guard enters handing a scanner to Scott before departing. Scott runs it slowly over Allmass, starting at his head, working his way down. Over the mid-section he gets a positive read. The scanner is picking up the radio frequency the microchip emits. He finishes going over Allmass's entire body before returning to the stomach region where he gets a positive read again. "He must have swallowed one." Scott says. "Voluntarily or not, not that it makes a difference. Want it out?"

Reggie silently taps your fingers on the chair's arms. "Leave it." She says.

"You sure?"

Reggie stops tapping and gives him the look. She doesn't like to be second guessed.

He notices. "Never mind." And moves back into his chair.

She resumes her quiet tapping and analyzing. "They'd have to know we'd find it…maybe. They could have been counting on Belette not having the forethought to scan him, he'd become incompetent because of his arrogance and Zach, whether he knowingly participated or not or shared any information, may not have known Felix is no longer in the picture."

"Makes sense." Scott replies before realizing she's in deliberation mode.

He's right, Reggie doesn't hear him as she continues, speaking to no one other than herself. "This means they don't know about this place specifically, they're simply looking for a lead on any one of the Committee's locations. So…this suggests Zach is not a cooperating participant otherwise he'd have told them. I'm sure he's playing every angle he can, he's that's the kind of guy but I don't think he'd have volunteered to come back here unless he had no other choice. And if he did, not this way, I'm sure." Reggie gets up and moves to her desk to grab her coffee, taking a couple sips before reaching for a breakfast bar. She's deep in thought, in her zone and starts pacing. "Logic says they were watching when Zach was taken and how long and by what method we came for him. Knowing it was by helicopter, they'd be able to establish an estimated radius from Ashford as to how far away we are." She turns to Scott. "They'll be in a vehicle…so that means we have a window of preparation of eight to twelve hours before they get here."

Scott sits quietly, not sure if he's suppose to respond in anyway. Reggie munches on the bar continuing to stare at him. "So, we're letting them find us?" Scott asks hesitantly.

"Absolutely." She replies between bites.

Allmass moves, groaning before massaging his head as he opens his eyes. "Where am I?' He hoarsely asks, still disoriented from the effects of the Midazolam. He slowly props himself up on his elbows, looking around and recognizes he's in Felix's office. Reggie approaches him. "What's going on…are you doing Belette's dirty work for him now?"

Reggie slaps him hard across the face again.

Zach winces in pain and rubs his cheek, "I have a feeling you did that to me before…miss you too." He says smiling. The two of them were close once, nothing serious but enough that they got to know each other pretty well. They kept it off the radar. "Where's Belette, still in his hole?" Reggie doesn't answer and takes a seat back in the lazy chair. Zach moves to an upright sitting position and looks over at Scott, "How about some water, I'm pretty dry?"

Scott grabs a bottle from Reggie's mini fridge, tosses it to him and Zach guzzles it down dropping the empty on the couch. He gives Reggie an appreciative look, "Wow, I forgot how good you look. Any chance you'll tell me how I got here?"

Reggie can't help but smile at the compliment. "Your friends in Rainier were nice enough to leave you on a bench in Ashford for the Sherriff to find. He knew you, so he called me."

"Why you? Where's Belette?"

"He…involuntarily stepped down. I've taken over." Reggie says.

"Wow, ambitious woman. I didn't realize you were looking to move up the corporate ladder. I thought you were smarter than that, had a conscious, one of the few here that actually did. I guess I was wrong." Zach says shaking his head in bewilderment.

"Don't look so disappointed. It may be to your advantage. You might be able to stay alive now." She says.

Zach sits back watching Reggie, looking for any sign of tell in her face, something he can get a read of but there's nothing.

"What happened, you weren't getting along with Smirnov and the Handlers?" She asks.

Zach chuckles shaking his head again, he's surprised and impressed she knows about the Handlers and Frank but tries not to let it show. Yea…something like that. Can't deny it, you were always good at figuring things out." Those sons of bitches dumping him in park, he never expected this from Frank but Willow? Yea, he could see her convincing Frank otherwise, especially after the stunt he pulled.

"Zach, honestly. You can't sit on the fence anymore. You have to choose."

"What, you're just going to let me back in, just like that?" Zach knows better. He does agree with her though, he needs to pick a side but he's far from ready for that.

Reggie starts her silent tapping on the arm of the chair again. "No, you'll have to earn your way, starting with telling me what you know about your friends. Then we'll go from there."

"Look, you probably already know what I know. Last thing I remember is driving around in a light brown Dodge minivan they'd just picked up. After that, it's a blur. I don't have a clue where they are."

Reggie smiles as she looks over at Scott.

"What?" Zach asks as he looks back and forth at the two of them, not sure what's so important about what he just said.

"That's a start and every bit helps but let's not assume what I may know." Reggie answers. "So begin."

CHAPTER TWENTY-FOUR

In her room at the lodge, Willow pulls out a very kinky cross between a laptop and a tablet and keys in the activation code for the microchip. It's been an hour since Zach was picked up from the Sherriff's office and she wanted to wait until it was absolutely necessary before initiating its signal as once it's on, it can't be powered down. The rest of the group is standing behind her watching and waiting.

Stogie peers down over her shoulder chomping down hard on his cigar, anxious for a location on the signal so they can get on the road. "It's working…looks like they're headed south to Northern California." He says stepping back so Oin can have a closer look. Frank doesn't bother, it's their equipment.

"Definitely. Based on their travel time, it can't be much further than that… unless," Oin says.

"Unless what?" Frank asks.

"Unless they're going to a different spot than where they started from." Willow pipes in as she closes her device. "Let's go. We'll continue this on road and hopefully get a hard location before they find the tracker, if they do. Let's keep our fingers crossed."

"Or hope we're not walking into something." Stogie adds.

"I know." Willow says. "I know."

"Why not just stay here and track it?" Frank asks.

"The range is limited even with our technology, three to four hundred miles at best in ideal conditions. We need to follow it to track it more precisely. Once we have a strong stable signal that's stationary long enough to confirm that's where Zach should be, we'll use your satellite systems to fine tune the location from there. Basically Google Maps to finish it off." Willow says.

"Makes sense." Frank replies. "Mind if I drive, I need to be doing something?"

"Good by me." Stogie says. "I'm sick of driving."

"All yours. I'm sure Willow won't mind the change of scenery from her co-pilot seat." Oin says smiling. Willow playfully backhands him in the chest for the comment. "What?" Oin laughs.

She walks out shaking her head, not daring to look back as she's blushing. Oin…he acts so much like a kid sometimes. I guess whatever works for each of them to get through this. "Now's not the time for games." She calls back trying to keep the mood serious even though she's looking forward to the improved view. They've been driving south on the I-5 for three hours when Willow directs Frank to pull over to a turnout.

"What's up?" He asks.

"The signal hasn't moved for a while now so I want us parked so I can get a location to verify where Allmass is at. It can get a bit intermittent when we're moving." Willow says. Oin jumps from the third row to the middle so he can get a better view and Stogie slides over to make room for him. "It's northern California alright, in the Klamath National Forest." She says as she waits for the satellite image to fine tune the location. "We'd have to go south a few more hours, turn west on route ninety-six…south on Klamath River Road…then south on Humbug Creek Road; ten miles in I'd guess."

"Looks pretty isolated," Frank comments.

"Let me switch from Google Maps to a satellite image." Willow says. The image hones in. "It looks like a private estate." And everyone crowds in for a peek.

"The main gates are just off the highway…and I would say that's a guard house just inside them." Stogie says pointing at the screen.

They image shows a vehicle at the gate and a couple of men mulling around but they know the image isn't recent. Willow pans back the view to check the rest of the grounds. It shows there's high brick fence that encompasses most of the grounds and quite elaborate landscaping to the property, it's a massive place. "Oh, there's the helipad." She says.

"There's going to be security camera's everywhere." Frank says. It reminds him of his place in Belize, the fortification of it, not the size.

"Patrolled around the clock, I'm sure." Willow adds.

"And dogs too, I bet." Oin says. "I don't like dogs."

"Let me make a call and let them know and I'm sure they'll accommodate you and switch to cats." Stogie says jokingly.

"Hey, thanks. Can you make it kittens then?" Oin quips back.

Stogie laughs. "I can just imagine."

"So, how do we approach this? We have the location but I think we still need to do a drive by." Willow says. "Confirm what we can in person."

"My gut says otherwise. We'd be heading down a secluded road with no alternative route out. We know they're well armed and equipped plus they have a chopper that can cut us off at anytime, assault of us from the air…there's a slew of scenarios that can do us harm." Frank says.

"That's if they know we're coming." Oin says. "I mean we can't be the only traffic along that road."

"You mean Frank coming. How would they know about us?" Stogie adds.

"How hard is it to detect that microchip?" Frank asks.

"It's high tech but…fifty fifty?" Willow says.

"They'd have to wonder why I dumped Zach and left him the way I did and not just kill him." Frank adds.

"If they had your pictures and Zach worked for them, odds are they'd know about you being school mates, that wouldn't be hard to dig up." Willow says.

Frank gives her a surprised look.

"Just because you didn't tell me, doesn't mean I don't know." Willow says to answer what she knows Frank is thinking. "Plus, would they even expect you to come at them solo?"

"It's probable they'll think you dumped him and ran. As far as they know you have the Orb safely tucked away with the Tsiatko. What reason would you have to go after them?" Stogie asks.

"We can go on our own Frank." Willow states.

Frank sits back. "Christ…I know and you're right. I just hate going in blind, has never been my style. But if I walk out on this I'll feel like such a chicken shit." He says. "And that's just not me. I have to remind myself what I'm here for in the first place. I'm supposed to make a difference."

Willow is trying not to say too much more as Frank's has to believe it's his choice to stay with them.

"It's not like we're going in defenseless. We loaded everything the two of you had when you left the cavern." Oin says thumbing to the back of the van.

Frank involuntarily looks up at Oin in the rear view mirror as if for a visual confirmation of the weapons. "You're right. We're just a minivan driving by. They can't even see inside this thing from the sides. Fuck it." Frank says as he throws it into gear and hits the gas.

Six hours and one pit stop later they slowly cruise by the estate. There's been no other traffic on this road since they turned on to it and that makes Frank feel exposed. Its dark which does offer them some cover but the grounds are brightly illuminated by assorted floodlights strategically placed everywhere. The signal from the microchip in Zach is strong and is being received loud and clear.

"He's still in there." Willow says as they continue past. "Well, the microchip anyways." She adds.

Frank drives a couple miles further pulling over onto the shoulder so he can make a U-turn. He looks over at Willow. "I don't like this." He says.

"Neither do I." She says. Oin and Stogie say nothing. They're watching the rear and the air for any signs of trouble.

"We do our final pass and then we're out of here, agreed?" Frank asks.

"Agreed," Willow replies.

They make their return pass, the manor is still quiet and there still is visible activity but the signal from the chip is gone. "We lost it." Willow says as she turns the screen towards Frank.

"That seems like too much of a coincidence. We'll find someplace to stay and figure things out from there." Frank says.

They get about five miles away before Willow pipes up. "Sorry Frank but I need you to pull over; I can't hold it any longer." She says.

"What?" Frank asks.

She's squirming in her seat. "I have to pee." She whispers. "We woman aren't like you men, we can't hold it forever."

"Can you wait til we get off this road?" Frank says.

"Frank…if I could I would but I can't. Don't expect me to sit here and wet myself!"

"Okay, okay." He says as he pulls over. "Hang on." And he makes sure the cabin light is off before she opens the door even though there's still no traffic anywhere to be seen.

Willow puts on her hat and gloves and zips up her coat.

"Where you going? Just go beside the van." Frank says.

Willow shakes her head at him. "Let a lady have some privacy? I'm just going to the edge of the trees." And she steps out.

"Well, if we're taking a bathroom break, I'll have one too but I'm staying by the van." Oin says smiling as he jumps out.

"I got the rear." Stogie says tossing the remains of his cigar on the ground as he gets out. "May as well, no use holding it if I don't have to."

Frank has the urge now too. "Christ." He says as he exits, electing to do what he needs to right on the highway. Moments later, he hears wood knocking. He quickly zips up taking a step to the rear just as the sky lights up and the three of them are engulfed by the spotlight from a helicopter above. The ground around them is sprayed with automatic fire, warning shots. "Shit!" Frank yells as he turns to get back in the van but more shots pepper the ground near him, halting him. Oin and Stogie haven't moved.

"Don't move!" a voice warns through the choppers public address system as it hovers fifty feet above them. "Any attempt to enter the van will be met with lethal fire!" It must be stealth mode equipped as its barely making a sound, Frank only feels a whirl of air coming from above. On the road, from both directions, three or four vehicles have turned on their headlights as they approach. They've been set up. It's a trap. Frank looks to the trees...Willow is nowhere to be seen. The three of them raise their hands in the air as the vehicles screech to a halt several feet away and a large force of armed men exit and approach. Some hold automatic rifles, others handguns. They disperse, a few assigned the task of searching them, others open the rear and side doors of the van, checking the interior.

"They're well armed!" One of them shouts out referring to the weapons cache in the back.

A smiling Garth Scott approaches Frank. "Well, literally caught with your pants down so to say."

"Fuck you." Frank replies.

"Where's the woman?" Scott asks.

"What woman?"

"Quit the bullshit. We know there were four of you. Where is she?" Scott demands.

"You know women. She didn't have the balls for the trip." Frank chuckles. "So we left her back at Rainier since we were only doing recon."

"I wouldn't keep talking that way if I were you, my boss, she wouldn't appreciate the comments." Scott warns.

"She?" Frank asks.

One of the crew approaches Scott showing him the high tech versions of the Taser guns. "We pulled these off the other two."

Garth takes one, examining it. He looks at Frank.

"Gag water guns, they're a riot." Frank says smiling. "Seriously, aim it at your head and try."

Scott aims it out into the ditch and pulls the trigger, nothing. He squeezes the trigger a couple more times with the same result. "Yea, imprinted." He mutters before tossing it back to the crew member. "Put them in the back with everything else." He says.

"Imprinted?" Frank wonders.

"Load them up!" Scott yells.

One of the team is aggressive and cross checks Frank hard from behind with his rifle to get him moving. Frank spins hitting him full force in the nose with the heel of his hand, driving it back into his brain. He drops dead onto the highway. Others approach him, weapons raised and he calmly stares back at them grinning, letting his eyes go dark and do the talking for him.

Scott calmly approaches shaking his head as he looks at the body on the ground. "Secure their hands…behind their backs and be nice about it, these are guests of Ms. Byrnes. And someone pick up this piece of shit, throw him in the van and follow us back in it." He orders. This done, Scott slides into the rear seat of an SUV beside Frank. Oin and Stogie are placed in another and they speed their way back to the estate.

Frank is thankful Willow wasn't found but worried at the same time. He wonders if the wood knocking was a warning that came too late.

CHAPTER TWENTY-FIVE

"How're you feeling Zach? You look a little peaked?" Reggie giggles as he emerges from the washroom, the sound of the toilet flushing in the background.

"What the hell did you give me? Zach asks. "I would've rather shoved my whole hand down my throat to get that microchip out."

"Let's call it partial payback." Reggie laughs. She'd given him a dose of Ipecac. It's like clear super sugary syrup with a bitter aftertaste that you wash down with a glass of water. Ten minutes later it activates an uncontrollable gag reflex that lasts for another five. Whatever is in your stomach comes up. She gave him a healthy helping just to make sure he suffered.

Zach stumbles his way to the couch, downing a bottle of water to get the taste of the Ipecac and vomit out of his mouth. "You're evil." He says resting his hand on his stomach. He looks at her seated in the lazy chair across from him. "Not that I'm looking my best right now but sitting here, seeing you again... I realize how much I missed you." He says.

Reggie raises her eyebrows at him. "Always trying to be the charmer, do you ever shut it off? Her playful mood has suddenly vanished as Zach has gone into a subject matter she'd rather not discuss.

Zach stares down at the water bottle, fidgeting with it. "When you said you were too busy with life to have a relationship, this," As he looks around, "Was not what I thought you meant."

"A woman has to take advantages of opportunities that are presented to her... Zach. Do you have any idea how much crap I've had to put up with in my life from men to get here? The constant petty remarks and ignorant attitudes from stupid, irresponsible degenerates that feel they're the most qualified to make all the decisions?" Reggie responds.

"I have to assume Belette didn't go willingly, you probably put him down like an old dog? I'm sure he didn't see that coming. I sure as hell didn't."

Reggie stands and walks over to him, crossing her arms, hovering over him. "There's a lot that men will not see coming. Things in this world are going to change." Reggie says heatedly before stopping herself. The emotions she rarely displays in public have taken control, she's said more than she wanted to.

Zach is taken back. "Wow, a side of you I haven't seen. That sounds like it's been pent up for awhile?"

Reggie drops her hands to her hips, bending down to Zach. "There's a lot about me you don't know Zach regardless of your past attempts at … prying. You shouldn't try and play in my field of expertise. A woman, more than anyone, is allowed to have secrets. You have a few as well it appears." Reggie says in a harsh whisper.

"What I did had nothing to do with us."

"Really?" Reggie asks as she stands upright and stretches her arms outward. "Look around where we are, your situation and who you're dealing with … I think it does."

"Ok … maybe now but I was always upfront with you about who I am, what I was and I did that only with you. My true intentions with the Committee … well, that's something different, that was outside the scope of our relationship."

Reggie returns to her chair, tapping the arm of the chair again. Her tell that she's in a state of deep thought. She waits a moment before replying. "Zach … that's the part you never did get. We didn't have a relationship. We had … a liaison of convenience. Friends with benefits if you must have a label for it." Reggie says flatly.

"That hurts." Zach replies.

Before the discussion can go any further, Bertram knocks and enters. "They're on their way back." He says referring to Scott and the team.

Zach looks back and sees the two guards still outside the open door as Bertram gives his update. It further fuels his apprehension, like he has a deadline he can't make. He's between a rock and a hard place. He's walking a fine line right now, still straddling the fence not sure which way to leap off is the best route for him and if he stays in the middle and slips, he could inflict a lot of damage to himself as well.

Reggie watches Zach's expression as Bertram makes the announcement, to see how he reacts. There's definitely concern on his part. Oh, she wishes she could trust him. It would make matters so much easier; she can't though regardless how she feels about him. She believes it's easier for women, unlike men, to let their minds override their feelings. Business is business and right now, there's too much at stake for games of the heart. "Bertram, contact all the secondary staff and notify them they have the next week off. I don't want anyone on premises other then us, the security detail and Scott's team, not until we're done with the transition. Before they leave, have the cooks prepare sandwiches and have them taken to the guest bedrooms in the east wing along with bottled water. We don't want our guests to go hungry; everyone else can prepare their own." Reggie says.

"Of course." Bertram says leaving.

Before Zach can say anything, Scott walks in. "I have them down in the vehicles, wasn't sure where you wanted them. Thought it was easier to just come up."

"Did you get them all?" Reggie asks.

"The woman wasn't with them."

"Anyone hurt?"

"None of them." Scott says.

Reggie sighs. "Put them all in the guest wing, separate bedrooms with a four person security detail on each one. We all need some rest. We'll continue this in the morning."

"And him?" Scott asks referring to Zach.

"Him too."

"Seriously?" Zach says as he stands.

Reggie gets up, removing the automatic she had tucked in beside the seat cushion.

"Really?" Zach says pointing to the gun. "That's the way things are now?"

Reggie approaches him with gun in hand, her breath warm as she comes in close and the scent of her takes him back to another time. She's well aware of the effect she has on him. "As dear as you may be to me … I'd rather be safe than sorry." She whispers, giving one last soft blow into his ear before stepping back.

Zach can't help but chuckle as he looks into her eyes. The mind game she's playing with him. Keeping him on his toes, not knowing what direction she's really headed. "You're the boss." He says.

"Yes, remember that." She replies as she crosses her arms again, resting the gun on her bicep.

Zach is escorted out but looks back at her as he exits. She's still watching him, she hasn't looked away. "That's a good sign, there may be hope yet." He thinks smiling.

Scott grabs a two-way radio from one of the guards at the door. "Bring them up to the east wing." He instructs the team in the vehicles. "You two," referring to the two guards, "Come with me and don't let this guy con you," Referring to Allmass, "He's not one of us anymore."

As they reach the east wing, they meet the group bringing up Frank, Oin and Stogie. It appears Frank and Zach will be in rooms across from one another. Frank stares at Zach as the plastic ties binding his hands are cut off. Once free, he massages his wrists to get the circulation going before giving Zach a cutthroat gesture. "Motherfucker." He says to Zach as he enters his designated room.

"Fucking asshole." Zach yells back at Frank as he enters his.

They each believe the other has betrayed him. Oin and Stogie don't say a word as they watch the drama, before setting foot in their accommodations.

Frank walks into what looks like a high end hotel room. The entire flooring is ceramic tile. He opens the full size closet, empty, not even a hanger. A king size bed sits in the centre decked out with high quality bedding. He's still a sucker for that. There's a small dining table for two, a computer work station, a large armoire that holds a decent size TV that's bolted down and a bar fridge that's secured in place. He's now feeling the pangs of hunger and pops open the fridge, it's empty. He checks out the washroom. It's a four piece complete with towels, a bathrobe, slippers and all the other amenities one would hope for; shampoo, conditioner, soap, a travel toothbrush, toothpaste, everything. He takes a moment to run cold water and uses one of the plastic cups wrapped in cellophane by the sink, to have a drink. He strolls back to the main room and over to the window, drawing back the drapes to check out the grounds and his options, to see full size windows … with security bars on the outside. So much for that possibility. He turns back around to survey the room. There's nothing than can effectively be used as a weapon.

Not even a coffeemaker or its carafe. Frank flops down on the bed to think things through. Wow, he can't help but appreciate how comfortable the bed is as he stares up at the ceiling. He's concerned about Willow, sure she's a Handler but she's still out there on her own. Does the Committee realize they've captured a couple Handlers along with him? He never got a chance to get Oin's and Stogie's take on things before they were carted off. He knows there are Tsiatko near but the knocking could've meant nothing, other than they're in the area. Expecting help from them would be an unrealistic long shot. Frank's kicking himself in the ass for stopping…he should've let her wet her pants. He can't believe they got the drop on him like that. He swings himself to the edge of the bed, too pissed off now to enjoy the comfort. He hears talk in the hallway and the door opens. Two guards enter in vests, M4's slung at their sides and Glocks strapped to their hips. Frank can see several more outside in the hallway. They aren't taking matters lightly.

"Stay there." One of them warns as the other sets a tray of sandwiches and a couple bottles of water on the table before they back out.

Frank sits and eats. He's starving and he knows he needs the nourishment. As he chews away, he's beginning to question Willow's plan of sending Zach back to the Committee. It seemed like a good stratagem at the time even though she wouldn't fully divulge what the rest of it entailed. He regrets not pushing for more details but he figured all he'd get was more half answers and he had no patience left for that…be should have, fucking hindsight, always twenty-twenty. He had tested the boundaries earlier on the highway when he killed one of the team, wanted to see how they'd react. There was no retaliation so obviously they mean him no harm, not yet anyways. He's at a roadblock trying to make sense of it all and has no avenues left other than to wait and see. He throws the remaining food in the fridge and has a shower, soaking in the refreshing hot water and after, elects to try and get some sleep. Eventually, it comes. He awakes with the sunrise, showers again and then pounds on the locked door.

"What?" Is the response.

"Hey, how about some coffee. You're killing me. This is cruel and unusual punishment." Frank says.

"Asshole." Is the only reply.

Ten minutes later the door opens and he's instructed to move by the window as another pair delivers two large Styrofoam cups and an assortment of packaged sugars and creamers. They leave in the same manner as the first pair and Frank is ecstatic to discover strong hot coffee in them. "What? No china? Where's the cream and sugar? No croissants or pastries? What kind of dump are you running here?" He yells out to entertain himself.

"Suck my dick." Is the reply.

Frank laughs. Eventually, out of boredom, he turns on the TV and finally finds a movie that interests him to pass the time. That one over, he starts channel flipping when the door opens. Two guards enter, weapons drawn followed by a very attractive woman who's flanked by two more armed men. She's a red head and she appears to enjoy the better things in life, based on how she's dressed. Frank's knows good quality clothing when he sees it. Frank stays sprawled out on the bed where he is.

"Morning Mr. Smirnov. It's good to see you're comfortable with your accommodations." Reggie says.

"Call me Frank. I did complain to the staff about the lack of delicacies and china with the coffee this morning but they didn't seem to care." He replies swinging his feet to the side of the bed to face her. "So I can only give you a three star rating now. This place definitely is not what your brochure said."

"Interesting, a hit man and a comedian." Reggie says, choosing not to mention she knows he's more than that.

"And who would you be?" Frank says standing. With that the two forward guards get in front of Reggie, aiming their guns directly at Frank's head. "Okay." Frank says sitting back down and the pair retreat slightly.

"I am your host, Reggie Byrnes."

"Where do you fit in with everything? I thought a guy named Belette runs the show."

"I'm his replacement. He's…no longer with us." Reggie smiles.

Frank wonders how literally he should take that. "Zach never mentioned you. I'd have to say, based on Zach's description of Felix, you're definitely better looking. I hope, less hostile than the Weasel." Frank says referring to Belette's nickname.

Reggie glances back at the closed door across the hallway before directing her attention back to Frank. "Don't let looks and my being a woman deceive you. I'd have to admit, I can be more ruthless. It depends on the circumstances and my patience."

"Not really what I wanted to hear." Frank says.

"Yes, well, I just wanted to introduce myself considering we'll be spending so much time together." Reggie says and immediately leaves before Frank can respond or ask about his travel companions. The guards wait til she exits before retreating and closing the door.

"My pleasure!" Frank yells. What the hell was that all about? No Belette? He wonders. "How long that has been? Was Belette ever the person Zach said he was? How much truth is there to any of Zach's stories?" Frank now believes he's been played, big time. He thought he was a smart guy however, he's feeling pretty stupid right now. He moves to the window. There're several guards patrolling the grounds…and not a kitten to be seen. He smiles and hopes Oin and Stogie are okay, Willow too. He hears the door open again and turns to see the four guards rushing him, their weapons at the ready. "Whoa, whoa," He yells putting his hands in the air. "I'm not doing a damn thing." They stop a few feet away with their guns still trained on him. "What? I'm doing shit, just standing here." One of the four lowers his weapon and unholsters a Taser gun. "Come on, you don't need that. I'll cooperate with whatever you need. You want my hands behind my back? I'll put them behind my back. I don't need any more tasering, okay? I've had enough of that crap. Just tell me what you want me to do." Frank pleads. The barbs from the Taser hit him full force and he drops. "Fuck!" He literally spits out as he's convulsing on the floor, his every muscle seemingly going into a spasm. He has that feeling of detachment and paralysis once more. The thirty seconds of voltage and constant pain feels like it'll never end. Then it's over, there's nothing left in Frank as they drag him off.

"Take him to the bunker." Scott says as they move past him in the hallway.

Reggie and another four of the crew are in Zach's room and Zach has been unfortunate enough to witness, through his now open bedroom door, what Frank has just gone through. Unfortunate because Zach has just realized he's about to undergo what Frank just did. "No, Reggie…come on." As he backs away from them."Look, I understand your concerns about Frank, he's dangerous. Me? I'll be gentle as a lamb. Seriously. I don't need to go through that shit." As he re-visualizes Frank's experience.

Reggie smiles, hands on her hips, she's loving every minute of it. "What? Not up to trying something new?" She asks.

"Fuck that! You made your point, loud and clear. Okay? If for some reason you think I wasn't taking you seriously… honestly, I am now." His arms are up in defense. It's no use, the barbs hit home.

Reggie saunters over as Zach convulses on the floor. Involuntary screams are coming out of his mouth as he goes through the same excruciating pain as Frank did. She looks down at his writhing body and giggles at Zach's suffering. "I'd still rather be safe than sorry." She says knowing he's oblivious to every word she's saying. "When he's done his dance, take him to the bunker to join the rest of them." She orders.

CHAPTER TWENTY-SIX

Reggie walks through the grounds to the bunker concealed behind a large grove of spruce. The access road to it, for vehicle traffic, follows a line of trees and is invisible from above. This is one of several bunkers the Committee has worldwide as temporary housing or as backup in case things get mismanaged. Yes, the optimistic view the Committee has on the world's survival Reggie thinks sarcastically as she ambles her way, they've given up on it a long time ago. These are not cold war era style facilities. They're luxurious accommodations designed for the wealthy and powerful, the elite. Some are family based; this one is for adults only. As she nears, she stops for a moment to survey this monstrosity buried into the rock hillside. Its drab grey façade holds hulking double hydraulic steel doors that create an airtight seal when closed. They're flanked by single person security door systems to take one through its nine foot thick insulated concrete core walls that can withstand temperatures to twelve hundred degrees. She traipses ahead and enters a security code giving her access to the one of the side entries. She strolls the three hundred feet through the garage and mechanical shop past a fleet of vehicles including luxury cars, Humvees and armored vehicles, parked on either side. As she walks, she looks up at the protective blast proof roof high above. This fortress can withstand a close range nuclear blast, a direct airplane crash, earthquakes, tsunamis, chemical and biological agents, EMP or any armed attacks, anything anyone could throw at it. She arrives at a duplicate set of doors to the first which are open and armed guards stand watch. Rather than the elevator she chooses to take the stairs to the primary level four stories down, she wants the exercise. As she progresses deeper, the ambience of the facilities becomes more luxurious and she exits to an expansive rotunda finished in decorative ceramic tile on the floors and walls, chandeliers, gold plated mirrors and handcrafted furnishings. She walks down the wide expanse of a hallway, past the opulent living area to her left and the lavish recreational room to her right. One would never imagine they were deep underground as LED screens strategically placed throughout as skylights give the impression of being above ground, programmed to represent sunny blue skies, cloudy days and other inclement weather. The windows are the same, providing illusions of city dwelling, the urban countryside, mountain views, the beach and a host of other available selections. She makes her way to the magnificent kitchen with its granite finishes and stainless steel appliances to find Scott seated at the elaborate island, on one of its many chrome and black barstools, sipping on a cappuccino. "Everything set?" She asks.

"Yea. I got them down in the mechanical wing in one of the unused storage rooms. Easier to clean up the mess after."

The bunker has a circular floor plan with a number of wings extending out like fingers from its hub. The mechanical wing stores the hybrid heat system, the self contained water and power generation systems, backup systems and storage facilities. The bunker is guaranteed to operate without any support from the outside world and accommodates twenty guests with a five year supply of food for each one.

Reggie reaches in one of the commercial fridges and grabs a bottle of San Pellegrino water. "I'm going for a walk before we get things started." She says, heading for one of the wings.

"I'll be here." Scott answers.

Three of the wings are home to twenty bedrooms with private washrooms, living areas and a dining area for those that want privacy. The TVs throughout the complex are linked to an extensive library of television programs, movies and video games that is constantly updated. Other wings contain an Olympic size pool, a full medical clinic, fitness facilities, a movie theater, an arcade, bowling alley and even a gun range as there's a well equipped armory on site. Reggie takes her time touring them all even though she's been through many times before. It's her way of slowing herself down; to make sure she's covered all the bases and hasn't overlooked anything before she gets the ball rolling. They only have one shot at this. If she fails, there's more at risk than antagonizing the Committee.

Frank feels like shit. His head feels…congested, like he took too much cold medication. Everything is a haze. Jesus, he's worried his mind is getting fried as this is the third time getting hit with high voltage in the last few months." He squints as he looks around. Not that it's bright; it's just easier on his eyes to focus. Things are blurry but beginning to clear. He's in some kind of small warehouse or storage area with empty steel racks scattered along the walls. Half a dozen men are lounging near the propped open double doors he's facing, none of them paying him much heed. Why should they, as he looks down, he's strapped to a fucking chair again. He looks over and sees Zach, Oin and Stogie are in the same predicament. Zach is still out of it, the other two seem alert.

"Hey, Frank, you okay?" Oin asks.

"Seriously? I've been tasered…again and I'm tied to a chair in, who knows where and you're asking me if I'm okay?" Frank says feeling more than a bit irritable.

"Well…yea, are you alright though?" Oin says.

"No!" Frank shouts. He's pissed. The guards turn with his outburst. "Fuck you too!" Frank yells at them.

"Suck my dick." One of them says laughing. It must be the same one that was outside his room.

Frank doesn't laugh in response this time and wiggles in his chair, trying to loosen the bonds even though he knows it won't help. "Uuuggghhh!" He shouts before taking a few deep breaths. It helps. He feels less…anxious, it clears his head a bit, giving room for a plan. "I need some water." He demands.

"Not a problem." Another guard says without hesitation, grabbing a large bottle from the floor. He uncaps it as he walks over, places a hand on Frank's forehead forcing his head back and dumps its contents into Franks open mouth. He continues with the unending stream even after Frank shuts his mouth to stop the cascade and the excess pours over Frank's face and front until the bottle is empty. "Enough?" the guard asks smiling. The rest of the men laugh.

Frank's eyes go dark briefly as he glares at his tormentor. "I'm going to fuck you up." Frank hoarsely hisses.

The guard's smile disappears. He swallows hard, placing a hand on his weapon as he backs away. The laughter in the background ceases.

Scott enters the room. It only takes him a moment to figure out what's just happened. He drifts the guilty guard a hard one across the chin and he hits the floor. "What the fuck is the matter with you?! I said nothing rough!" He shouts. There's no response from his men. "Any of you do anything again; I will literally rip your heads off!" Scott is one scary looking mother and none doubts his threat. He walks over and looks down briefly at the soaked Frank.

"Hey, I forgot to tell you before, love the hair." Frank says. At this point Frank's out to antagonize this bunch, hoping someone will make a mistake, that's the only shot he's got.

Scott continues on, lifting the chin of the still incognizant Zach to check him before moving over to Oin and Stogie. "You two okay? Scott asks them.

Oin and Stogie look at each other. "We're good." Stogie says. "I'd be better if you dig a cigar out of my shirt pocket for me?"

Scott doesn't comply and walks away, scowling at his men as moves past them exiting the room. The minutes drag on in silence before Zach finally moves. As he becomes more alert and aware of the situation, he struggles to free himself of his bonds.

Frank would like to shout out and curse him but he knows it's his own fault for being in this situation. He's the one who went along with Willow's plan and the trek to find this place even though his gut told him different. "Hey Suck My Dick Guy." Frank calls out. "My friend here looks thirsty, how about giving him a drink the way you gave me one?" Frank says raising his eyebrows, winking but his request is ignored. "C'mon, Suck…My…Dick…Guy, your boss, the one with the really groovy hair by the way, said to treat us nice remember?" Frank winks a few more times.

Suck My Dick Guy reluctantly walks to Zach and gently provides him a drink, not in the manner Frank was hoping for. "You're a shit head." Frank says and is rewarded with splashes of water from Suck My Dick Guy's water bottle. "I'm tellin." Frank quips like he's a school kid, still trying to goad them.

Zach looks over at Frank. He's not forgiving like Frank about their predicament. "Way to go asshole, like being tasered and tied up again?"

"Can someone tape this guy's mouth close?" Frank yells. "There's not supposed to be talking during the movie. What's the feature today? I hope not

Woman in Red… I've seen that way too many times." Frank smiles and laughs looking over at his fellow captives. Oin and Stogie can't help but laugh along.

"Your brain IS cooked this time." Zach says seriously.

Frank starts wiggling his butt in the chair. "Hey, Water Bottle Boy, help me out here. I got his itch in my crotch that I can't quite reach. You look like you have small girly man hands, help a guy out here." Frank chuckles. He sees he's getting to them but they ignore him. "Okay, any of you guys then?! You all look like you'd enjoy it?!" He shouts.

Oin is beside himself laughing and Stogie is snickering which adds to the guards' frustration with Scott's no touch order.

"Frank, shut the hell up." Zach says, not understanding Frank's intentions.

"Why, we might get hurt? I think we're pretty much fucked Zach, you included even if these are your people, so shut the fuck up, I'll run my mouth off anyway I want." Frank orders. "I will, because I have now learnt that the one thing I hate more than anything is being tasered and tied to a fucking chair!" Frank yells.

"Not that I care to argue but you aren't going to like what's coming next even more. It's not going to be like last time. They're not going through all this just to kill us. No… they're going to torture the crap out of us first, suck every last bit of information they can and they'll take their time about it … then kill us. So, great plan you came up with you son of a bitch … fuck you're stupid." Zach says shaking his head.

Water Bottle Boy and Suck My Dick Guy laugh along with the rest of the crew at Zach's insult to Frank.

"Hey, if you guys really want a good laugh, come on over and take my seat. Let's trade places and you can let me know how hysterical this is." Frank says. "Besides, I'm really starting to cramp up and can use the stretch … no? Fine … Water Bottle Boy, come over here with those girly hands and give my shoulders a rub then, get them loosened up for me. There's a twenty dollar tip in my front pocket. I'll let you dig it out?" Frank teases looking over at his comrades again laughing. Frank's impressed by the hold Scott has on his men. He can see they want to bite but are holding back. They're definitely more afraid of Scott than taking their exasperations out on him. "No? How about fifty then? You get to go through both front pockets." Frank says smiling, raising his eyebrows and winking but there's no reaction from them. When Scott re-enters, Frank knows his hopes of creating some kind of escape opportunity are over.

Scott now has a silencer equipped M4 cross slung over his shoulder and has a two way radio strapped to his belt beside a holstered automatic. It appears, by the way his jacket pockets are shaped and hanging, he's carrying spare clips for the carbine as well. He looks like he's prepped for a fire fight. He saunters over to Frank. "I hear you like electric devices." Scott says smirking. "Hey!" He shouts to his men. "Bring me a portable battery charger from the garage; we're going to have some fun." And one of them leaves to complete the task. "I said THEY couldn't do anything to you." Scott adds.

Zach bows his shaking head, dreading what he knows is coming. Frank looks over at Oin and Stogie; they're quiet as mice, looking down at the floor. No one utters a word for several minutes, not even Frank. The bound and tied group's attention is brought back to life by the guard wheeling in the charger.

What the fuck, there's nothing fucking portable about that Frank thinks as the unit is brought in, it must be for a Goddamn tank. He nervously looks up at Scott who has remained standing over Frank the entire time.

Scott grins seeing Frank's expression as the charger arrives. "You like?" Scott asks.

"No…not one fucking bit." Frank replies. Where's his damn Power now and Fate when he needs its intervention so badly? So much for saving this damn world.

"I didn't think so. Get some juice into that thing, there's an outlet over there." Scott instructs his men, referring to the wall behind Frank. Moments later Frank hears the hum of the charger and smells sulphur in the air, it's so close behind him. When Scott briefly touches the two large alligator clamps together, not only does the sound of the sudden spark of high voltage resonate in Frank's ears, the hair on the back of his neck stands up due to the extreme electrical discharge. "That'll do just fine." Scott says, powering it down. He comes in close behind Frank "I bet you can't wait?" Scott whispers.

Frank's done with the smartass routine and keeps his mouth shut.

Scott laughs as he makes his way to the door.

Suddenly over the two-way Reggie is calling. "I need everyone in the bunker now, we have a security breach. Do you hear me? Everyone, now!" She demands.

Scott grabs his radio. "Repeat."

"We have a breach, everyone not in the bunker, get here now, we need support!" She orders.

Scott places his radio on a shelf, cranking the volume up so he can hear any transmissions. "Close those doors." He orders his men as he moves back into the room. "Keep your eyes and weapons on the doors, don't let any hostiles in." Through the radio shouts, screams and constant weapon fire can be heard. Water Bottle Boy looks back at Scott. "Don't look at me, watch the damn doors!" Scott yells. A battle is raging on somewhere in the bunker and is coming through the transceiver loud and clear. The screams amid the gunfire are almost inhuman and Scott's men nervously glance back and forth at each other, their weapons aimed at the entry. Suddenly Scott opens fire emptying his full extended mag into his crew…they never had a chance. Scott moves forward as he re-loads silently indicating to his four captives to be quiet. Frank, Zach, Stogie and Oin are in shock by Scott's actions and don't hesitate to keep still. Scott methodically empties another clip into the bodies strewn on the cold cement. He lowers his weapon, quickly going through the clothing of his team and removes their cell phones. He breaks each one open, removing the SIM cards and splitting them apart. This complete he pulls two scanners from his back belt. One is a Radio Frequency Detector for scanning radio and GPS based electronic devices, the other a Nonlinear Junction Detector for semiconductor electronics. He runs both of them over the bodies. Satisfied, he picks up the now quiet two-way, "All clear." He announces setting it back down. He starts dragging the bodies away from the door, resting them against the empty racking. This task done, he props the doors back open. He turns to his captives and puts a finger across his lips, reminding them to be silent as he backs into the hallway and waits. What seems like several minutes later, a well armed Reggie and Bertram parade in followed by Scott with Brother and Gaylord bringing up the rear, like they're one big happy extended family. Frank sees several other Tsiatko out in the hallway.

Willow steps out from behind Gaylord, "Hello Frank. Miss me?" Willow asks.

CHAPTER TWENTY-SEVEN

What the fuck is this? Frank wonders as he watches Bertram walk over to Oin and Stogie and cuts their binds.

Zach looks at Frank, almost reading his mind. "I haven't a clue." Zach says.

Bertram frees Zach before Frank. Frank remains seated while the other three get out of their chairs. He sits watching the oddball group in front of him as they watch him.

Oin and Stogie move over to Willow. "That went pretty smooth." Oin says grinning as Gaylord gently pats him on the shoulder.

"Like clockwork." Stogie adds as he pulls out a cigar and starts chomping down on it, Willow nods and smiles glancing at Frank as she does.

Zach walks behind his chair and leans on its backrest, not sure what to make of it all or what to do. Frank bows his nodding head. It's beginning to sink in that he was a pawn. Just a piece in the game that this outfit used to reach a means to an end and…he doesn't like it, he's feeling the fool. He pushes himself out of the chair, twisting and stretching his neck and takes a position similar to Zach's behind his own chair. Zach's not looking too impressed about matters either. The two of them watch and wait in silence.

Willow approaches Frank. She can see he's hurt, trying to hold it in. "Frank, I'm sorry but it's not about you. It's about the world." She says sincerely.

A single tear involuntarily runs down his cheek. He feels betrayed, used, embarrassed…things he hasn't felt since he was a kid and she gently wipes it away. He's not feeling much like the man he thought he was, at the moment and looks down. Willow places her hand on his head and gives it a soft stroke.

Zach turns to face the wall, crossing his arms as he leans lightly back on the chair. His feelings are similar as he now knows he was used as well. He's not feeling very jubilant about being free at this moment. No one comes to comfort him.

Frank takes a couple big breaths. He knows he has to push past his feelings and suck it up. He looks up. "Why the big charade?" He asks.

Willow looks back at the group and over at the dead bodies piled up. "Let's go someplace more hospitable to talk." She says.

Reggie leads the way. They are a sight, several humans followed by the Tsiatko as they proceed down the wing and into the kitchen where Brother instructs most of the Tsiatko to remain. The rest of the group continues to the living area.

"Quite the digs." Frank says sarcastically as he looks across at the rec room before following them into the living area.

"Get use to them, this'll be your new home for awhile." Reggie says.

"Frank stops. "What do you mean?"

"We'll get to that." Willow interjects. "Sit…please."

Frank gazes at the imitation skylights with their forged exterior views and the pure over the top luxury before sitting down on one of the several couches in the room. The rest take various spots except for Brother and Gaylord who remain standing. Zach chooses one that places the greatest distance between him and Reggie and it doesn't go unnoticed. "Well." Frank says as he looks around the room before studying Willow. "Put it all together for me because…I don't have a clue. I mean, what're you doing working with the Committee and how did you con him?" Indicating Brother, "Or is it part of the same trap you laid for me way back at Rainier? Christ." Frank gets up, shaking his head, rubbing his face again. "There's no way you could have pulled this off without Zach's help." He faces them all, his arms out stretched. "Am I the only one not in on this?"

"Frank, I had nothing," Zach begins.

Willow turns to Zach, pointing at him. "Shut up!" She demands before returning her attention to Frank. "They're not the Committee, they're Handlers."

Zach jumps up. "Bullshit to that! Jesus, I worked for them! I know who the Committee is and who's not! What kind of crap is this?!"

Willow rises and faces Zach. "Rein it in! This explanation is for Frank, not you! Your fate is still up in the air!" She warns him.

Zach receives cold stares from Oin, Stogie and Bertram, a threatening look from Scott while Reggie's face is emotionless. Brother and Gaylord do not give him the time of day so he reluctantly sits back down.

Willow turns to Frank, "They're a team just like us. We didn't know they were here until recently. Like us, they weren't prepared to give up. Their methods," Willow says nodding to Reggie before looking back at Frank, "Are more… aggressive and they chose to go in a different direction than us by infiltrating the Committee itself. Zach's actions were all his own… that is, until we sent him back to Reggie." Willow says.

"And as for Willow's team, we didn't know they were here either until Willow contacted me. Well, sort of didn't know." Reggie says smirking. "I didn't recognize any of them but when I used facial software on an ATM picture of Oin and got hits going back a few centuries, I knew. Willow got a hold of me shortly after. She already had a plan of her own in place but after some discussions, we made some modifications and here we are." Reggie states.

Frank sits. "Nothing's that simple. How'd you find out about the other team?" He asks Willow.

"At the Sherriff's office when they came to get Zach. Unlike Oin, Scott has a way of standing out, someone you would remember." She smiles.

Frank sees these two teams of Handlers are right at home with each other. Why shouldn't they be.

Willow continues. "The guy's wouldn't have recognized him without binoculars, he was too far away and moving too fast. I needed to be sure so I got a hold of Reggie. It's a simple process to reach out to another Handler when you need to."

Frank watches all their faces as Willow speaks. Their story has credence and he can see it in their eyes. Frank's feeling a little less defensive, foolish and hurt. These Handlers have thousands of years of experience and frustrations invested in this process. Him, he's playing it by ear. He may have been created in earlier times during previous occupations but all memories of those died with his each of his passings, with each of the failures. "And the Tsiatko?" Frank asks.

Willow walks to Brother. "The night I had Oin be there for you with the van and after you left for Seattle, I went searching in the cavern for the Tsiatko. I announced who I was and they came. It didn't take much to convince him I was a Handler. Once they accepted that fact, they were more concerned as to what I could do to them as opposed to what they could do to me." Willow says, placing her hand on Brother's arm to demonstrate as much respect as she can as she speaks of their arrangement. "We talked about what we both wanted for this planet and our passion for its continued existence. We negotiated terms, part of which was allowing you and Zach to escape. We also made a pact to work in harmony against the Committee and to do what was required to preserve this place for all life. So with the Tsiatko's help, we've made it this far."

"Great, everyone is working hand in hand, Kumbaya and all that. But for what? What's the end game? I still don't understand why the pretense and the masquerade…why slaughter everyone?" Frank asks.

It's Reggie's turn to speak up and she stands to do so. "Why? It's because the Committee was watching Belette like a hawk. They're watching everyone especially after Zach went AWOL." She says looking over at him. "And I'm sure they have me under a microscope. We had no idea as to the extent of their surveillance, satellite, bugs, video…spies, so we had to make everything, every detail, action, discussion seem legit. The only place that's secure, is in here." Reggie leans back against a wall, crossing her arms. "You call it slaughter; I call it starting with the required clean slate."

Frank turns back to Willow. "And you're good with this?" He looks around, "You're all okay with this? Shit…I don't even know why the hell am I even asking that question?" He says.

"You're right, you shouldn't ask, actions speak louder than words." Willow says as the others simply nod. "A big part of this is protecting you. We will now have DNA from bodies including yours to prove there was a battle led by you that took out insurgents who had infiltrated Felix's security teams and that the risk from Frank Smirnov, the dreaded hybrid, has now been eliminated. All thanks to Zach's covert scheme of befriending an old school mate. Well, that's what Reggie will let the Committee believe. With no witnesses to dispute Reggie's version of events, it will further elevate her status and let her continue to move up the ranks of the Committee while giving you someplace safe and secure to live."

"And you think this is the best route to go?" Frank asks disparagingly.

Willow moves toward Frank. "You know why we have failed for so long, so many times? I had to look down deep for the answers. It' because of men. Always trying to run the show, more worried about who had the bigger dick, rather than getting the job done right the first fucking time. Excuse my French but I'm," She looks at Reggie, "WE"RE sick and tired of it. We love the men on our teams." She says as she scans their faces, "But even they know we're right. These damn occupations, the playbook for these…experiments, written by men, directed by men and every one a damn failure."

"As I move up," Reggie adds to the discussion, "I'm taking Willow and her team with me. We're going to take down the Committee from the inside and we Handlers, led by women are taking over the show."

"And there are more of us, other Handlers floating around out there in space because they don't know what to do with themselves, with a wait and see attitude about what transpires here. We're bringing them all back." Willow says. "There WILL be fruit from our labors."

She could be one hundred percent right but whether it's men or women, Handler or human, to Frank it sounds like it could be easily become a dictatorship. "And what, men become second rate citizens?" Frank asks.

Willow looks like she's going to explode. "Second rate?!" She pokes her finger hard into Frank's chest. "My point exactly! When women are in that role, no problem! We want to put men in it, now its second rate?!" I thought you were better than that?!" She shouts.

"That's not what I meant." Frank says trying to back pedal. Willow only stares him down. There's a side of her that has emerged that Frank didn't see coming. His manhood is taking a hit again and he's not sure how good he'll be at swallowing his pride, taking orders, not being in control. If he does, will he ever be able to reclaim it? Frank changes the topic slightly, hopefully to his benefit. "You said this is going to be my home. It sounds like it's could end up being more like a prison. What exactly am I suppose to be doing here?" He asks.

Willow turns to Brother who gives instructions in his native tongue to Gaylord. He leaves and they all wait for several moments for his return. He's carrying a satchel which he hands to Willow. She sets it down on a coffee table and gently removes a wrapped object which she places in a large glass dish in the centre of its surface. She reveals the Orb. "You're going to start earning your keep, your choice of course." She announces smirking "And learn to sync with the Orb."

"And Zach, what's to become of him?" Frank asks wondering and hoping he'll be of some value, even though the warning from Mr. H still haunts him. "Trust no one."

"Leave him to me." Reggie interjects. "Don't worry; he'll be kept alive, earning his keep as well … maybe not as voluntarily as you." She says. Zach looks up at her, unsure whether he should be excited about that news.

EPILOGUE

Frank has the Orb set up in the rec room of the bunker. He's trying to get the knack of working with it, learning to co-exist with it and experimenting with it as much as he can. Oin is lounging on one of the couches, munching and watching a movie oblivious to what Frank's doing, as the intrigue of the Orb has worn off for him. Frank lets him hang out here when Oin needs to get away from the rest of the Handlers. They're busy doing their thing, Frank is left to do his and he prefers it that way. There are no prying eyes watching his progress and Oin swore he wouldn't share anything he saw. Oin seems to be caught up in the middle now, not sure what side of the so called fence he wants to be on.

Suddenly Gaylord merges through the wall. "Christ Gaylord," Frank says as he lets go of the Orb. "How many times do I have to repeat myself? When you enter a room, you have to announce yourself. Privacy, remember? We talked about this." Frank says.

"Brother, I'm sorry." Gaylord says sheepishly. He's still Frank's assigned Tsiatko bodyguard.

"Never mind, you're in here already, go hang with Oin or something." Frank instructs him.

Gaylord makes his way to Oin and takes a seat. Through trial and error he knows what furniture can take his weight.

"How you doin?" Oin asks him.

"I am doing well." He answers. "I have been thinking though," As he leans in close to Oin. "Willow, she is a strong woman, a good leader. She will make an ideal mate for my Brother Frank." He whispers loudly, too loudly. "He needs someone. He spends too much time alone."

Oin shakes his head no.

"What? Aren't these the very words you shared with me?" Gaylord asks.

Oin glances at Frank as he quickly sits up. "Dude, remember what I said about just between us?" Oin reminds him.

"Oh yes, I forgot." Gaylord replies.

"I can hear you!" Frank shouts. "Don't go there please! Not something I want to hear or discuss!" He says, sounding irritated as he struggles to getting back to where he was with the Orb before Gaylord intruded.

Oin raises his hand in acknowledgement. "Sorry Frank."

Moments later Zach knocks on the doorway as he enters. "Hey Frank, how's it going?" He says as he walks past and stands by Oin and Gaylord. Obviously Zach is escaping Reggie again.

Frank's still trying to figure out what kind of relationship they have. Working, personal or a combination of both. He knows neither of them trusts the other. Frank doesn't envy his circumstances. Christ, Frank thinks as Zach walks by… he thought he'd at least have some privacy here but it seems like its becoming more like Grand Central Station.

"What's the movie?" Zach asks Oin, quickly reaching in to a large bowl to grab a handful of buttered popcorn that Gaylord is devouring.

"Woman in Red." Oin teases.

"I heard that too!" Frank shouts.

"Actually it's Harry and the Hendersons." Oin laughs.

"Cute movie." Zach says. "Relative of yours?" He asks Gaylord. Gaylord gives him a blank look, he doesn't get the joke. Zach starts to walk over to see what Frank's up to when, from under the table where Frank's working, a strange creature comes semi shuffling out towards him. It's the size of a medium dog and looks like a cross between a Shar-Pei and a caterpillar. "Jesus. What the hell is that?" Zach yells moving to the side. Besides its puckered body, it has eight wrinkly short legs and each limb has a half dozen evil looking claws protruding from the end of it. Its eyes are tiny round black dots and it has a big rumpled snout of a mouth, if he can even call it a mouth as it looks more like an extended suction cup. The creature turns in Zach's direction so he back pedals and ends up plopping onto a couch as it approaches nearer. Oin and Gaylord have seen it often enough, so they pay it no mind.

Frank turns to look. "Oh," As he checks back under the table. "Didn't know he was running around. That, my friend, is a Water Bear." He says nonchalantly.

"A what?" Zach exclaims as it inches closer to him.

"Well, officially they're called Tardigrades. They're a microscopic type of creature that was first discovered here in the seventeen seventies. Scientists have suggested they're an alien life form that can withstand virtually anything. Extreme heat, bitter cold, can go without food or water for years, radiation hundreds of times higher than what would be lethal to us, survive an asteroid impact and even live in outer space they've speculated." Frank says brushing his hands on his pant legs. "It's all true and there are millions of them on this planet."

"Hate to tell you this Frank." Zach exclaims, "This ain't a microscopic creature." As he swings his legs up on the couch as it reaches him.

"It isn't. The Handlers originally brought them here from Mars but left them in a shrunken state. They're harmless that way. I found a way through the Orb to restore them to their original size. They're kind of cute… in their own way." Frank says as he kneels to gently pet it.

Zach cautiously reaches out from his perch to do the same. He's amazed as to how soft it is. It looks like it is covered in bare skin but it has a really plushy silky feel to it. It's making a strange whirring thrum sound as Frank and Zach pet it, like its purring and it starts to rub itself against the fabric of the furniture extending its snout upward.

"Careful." Frank warns.

"What?" Zach asks leaning back.

"Its snout. If it latches on, it's tough to get off." Frank says.

"What happens if it does?"

"Considering these things live only on liquids and our bodies are seventy percent fluids, I'd estimate it'd have you sucked dry in about four minutes… maybe five." Frank states.

Zach jumps over the back of the couch. "And you let it get that close to me? What're doing with screwing around with them?"

Frank gives him a sly smile. "You don't want to know." He whispers as he grabs the Water Bear by a fold of its skin and leads it away.

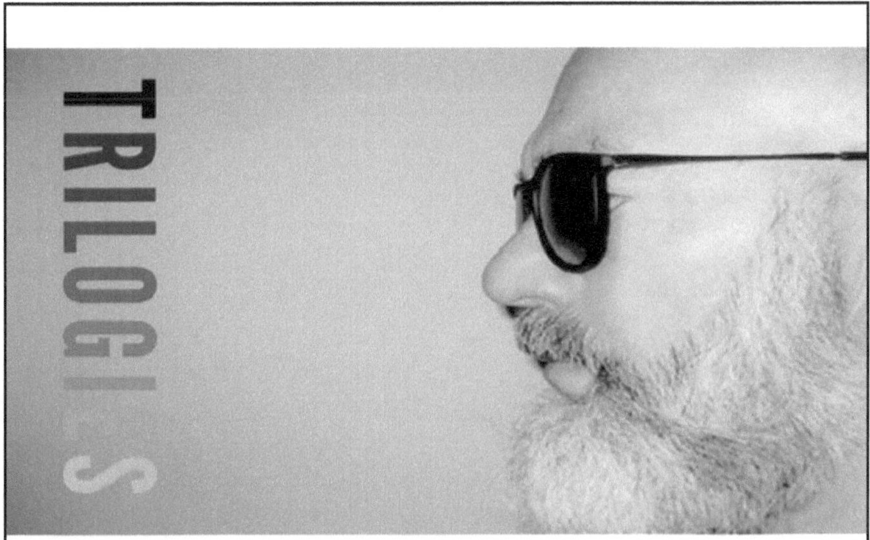

THE XENO MANIFESTO

THE XENO MANIFESTO – RECLAMATION

THE XENO MANIFESTO – REDEMPTION

Website – www.brysenmann.com
Instagram – brysenmann
Twitter - @brysen_mann
Facebook - @brysenmann